ALMOST FIRED BY THE COWBOY

MILLER BROTHERS OF TEXAS BOOK FOUR

NATALIE DEAN

DEDICATION

*I'd like to dedicate this book to YOU! The readers of my books.
Without your interest in reading these heartwarming stories of love,
I wouldn't have made it this far. So thank you so much for taking
the time to read any and hopefully all of my books.*

*And I can't leave out my wonderful mother, son, sister, and Auntie. I
love you all, and thank you for helping me make this happen.*

Most of all, I thank God for blessing me on this endeavor.

Copper Creek Romances Series 2

Making a Cowgirl

Marrying a Cowgirl

Christmas with a Cowgirl

Trusting a Cowgirl

Dating a Cowgirl

Catching a Cowgirl

Loving a Cowgirl

Marrying a Cowboy

Callahans of Copper Creek Complete Collection

KEAGANS OF COPPER CREEK

Copper Creek Romances Series 3

Some Cowboys are Off-Limits

Some Cowgirls Love Single Dads

Some Cowboys are Infuriating

Some Cowboys Don't Like City Girls

Some Cowboys Heal Broken Hearts

Some Cowgirls are Worth Protecting

Some Cowboys are Just Friends (Coming August 2024)

Though I try to keep this list updated in each book, you may also visit my website nataliedeanauthor.com for the most up to date information on my book list.

CONTENTS

1

Salvatore

*I*t is unfortunate that you've gotten the impression
we've—

No, that was too combative, putting the blame on them for
having a bad impression. Deleting it, Salvatore tried again.

*I assure you that the McLintoc Miller brand is still on course
and united—*

No, that was a blatant lie, and one that was easy to
disprove.

Growling, Sal slammed his laptop shut, his desk groaning
in response as he pushed himself away.

He *hated* writing emails, he hated sales, and he was pretty
sure he hated his brothers for getting him into the mess in the
first place.

But *noooo*, Solomon had to get up on whatever fancy horse
he was on and refuse to work with one of their long-time

contracted companies that they sold manure to. Something about harmful chemicals? Or worker abuse? Sal couldn't keep track. It seemed like every week his brother was trying to save the world this way, or improve morale that way, and he just couldn't stand it anymore.

Sal had liked the way things were *before* his family had started falling apart. He wasn't quite sure how it had happened, but one minute Samuel announced he wasn't coming back home, and the next minute, three of his other brothers had turned into some bleeding heart, environmental mumbo-jumbo-touting enthusiasts.

He didn't get it.

Sure, things hadn't been perfect, and sure, Sal had been a periphery son at that, fit for errands and any task that needed intimidation. But he'd been *fine* with that. He liked his family's lifestyle. He appreciated how hard his father had worked to build their ranching empire, and he *didn't* appreciate how his brothers were beginning to sound like poor folks, always blaming someone else for their problems. Never willing to take responsibility and always wanting handouts...

His temper spiked up again and then he was on his feet, walking from his wing to the kitchen. Sure, maybe food wouldn't cure his problems, but it sure wouldn't hurt. Besides, it wasn't like he wouldn't work it off in the gym later.

Then again... he had a *lot* less gym time since he'd started taking over multiple responsibilities from his brothers. Because hey, if they were going to jeopardize their position in the family, at least Sal could take advantage of it.

... he just wished those responsibilities involved fewer emails. He never was very good at writing. Gym class had certainly been his strong suit.

If only life was as simple as it were in high school.

Granted, when he'd actually been that age, Sal had been the smallest and reediest of all his siblings. Even Simon had stood at least a couple of inches taller and broader than him. But he'd finally hit the standard Miller growth spurt in his senior year, and then he got involved in bodybuilding, and *then* he hadn't stopped growing until he was twenty-three.

Sometimes, Sal still saw himself as that tiny boy, the smallest of all his brothers. Now he was the biggest, but that didn't seem to earn him much respect.

It didn't help that Simon was still off on his world-traveling thing. *That* had been a real wild fight, right in the middle of Simon's graduation party. Sal was pretty sure that his younger brother had done that on purpose, as the furor stopped pretty much everyone from addressing him directly.

As it were, his cousins to the north and cousins to the west had cut off almost all of their contact with Dad. They didn't bother to talk to Sal much either, but he wasn't sure if that was because he never was close with them or because they knew he was trying to help Dad keep the business on track.

Besides, he'd never really liked the western cousins. One son and four daughters from the youngest brother on his Dad's side, and they were all... grouchy? Sal wasn't sure that was the right word for it, but there was a certain standoffishness to them. Like they were always judging his family for everything.

He reached the kitchen, wondering if any of Mom's pecan pie was still left. But as he walked through the open door, he realized that one of the twins was there with all three of the low-class women who seemed to have invaded the ranch as of late. The tiny, trampy one, the redheaded mechanic who needed to wear looser clothing, and the tall veterinarian who needed to smile more. Sal had heard his dad rant about them at length, and he couldn't help but wonder if the three were part of some sort of coordinated effort to ruin his family.

Granted, they didn't look particularly conniving at the moment. It looked like Teddy was teaching Silas the "proper" way to make a grilled cheese, and Elizabeth was laughing lightly at the lecture. Mom and Frenchie were just outside the door, washing something he couldn't see with a hose, seemingly having a great conversation.

In some very small way, he understood it. All three of the women, as different as they were, were quite pretty. They'd been around enough for him to observe some of their quirks and personalities, which made sense when matched up with his brothers, in a way.

There was the Frenchie girl, who was bright and animated and was always trying to draw something. He saw how she brought his brother Solomon out of his shell, coaxing him to have more fun and not dedicate his whole life to the job. Also, Sal had been there when they'd chased the girl down, and she had an edge to her. Something strong enough to stand up to Solomon when he was so sure that he was right.

Then there was the mechanic, Teddy. She was actually fairly useful on the ranch, back when she'd worked there on weekends, and she still occasionally helped them out when they needed it. She was a bigger girl, with curves that were evident even through her mechanic's uniform. It was easy to see why Silas couldn't keep his eyes off of her, especially considering that he'd never dated anyone after his disastrous first relationship in college.

And then there was... *Elizabeth.*

She was the one that Sal had to deal with the most often, and she was the one that he always tried to avoid. She was cold, direct, and demanding. She told people, rather than asked, and he only ever saw her smile when she was talking to Sterling or other people in her little cluster of revolutionists. She rubbed him the wrong way, and he thought it would do her well to be warmer toward him, considering his family was employing her. But that same steel is probably what made her bring Sterling to life. Sal had always gotten along with the younger twin in his family, but the guy had been about as directionless as a dead lily pad in a river. His sudden drive would have been an improvement, if he wasn't busy using it to be a thorn in their father's side.

Maybe Sal was even jealous. He'd dated plenty, occupying his weekends with fling after fling. Never going very far beyond some kissing and light canoodling. Sure, he'd been tempted plenty of times, but then his mother and all she had taught him would pop into the back of his head, and all of the rushing blood stopped rushing and left him with a sinking stomach.

Would he like to date someone long-term? To be as contented and excited as his brothers seemed about their gals? Sure. Maybe. It looked nice. But of all the girls he went on dates with, there was never really a connection. They were just soft, pretty women that were nice to kiss, but that was about it. The way his brothers looked at their loves, he could tell that they really *felt* something toward their partners. Even if it was making all of them sound insane.

But then Silas looked over his shoulder, catching Sal's gaze and the tension in the room ramped right up.

"Hey," the older twin said slowly. "How're you?"

It was an olive branch, Sal could tell that much, but it just made him angry. It was easy for his older siblings to pretend they were some knights in shining armor, saving fair damsels from the big bad corporation, but they were delusional. They were caught up in their own egos, imagining that they were grand heroes.

"Save it," Sal said, turning on his heel and heading back to his office to try at that email again.

They were definitely a house divided, but he didn't see it fixing itself anytime soon.

2

Nova

$\mathcal{N}$ova was so excited that she was totally nauseous.

It wasn't the best reaction, but she was so unused to good things happening to her that she felt like her blood was racing in her own veins. It was her first day on her new job, and it was a job that she'd worked *so* hard towards that also paid well.

Which, basically, was an impossible combination.

And yet there she was, following behind her tall, commanding employer as the vet gave her a full tour of the ranch that she was supposed to be helping on.

"And this is the vet station that we're building. Obviously, it's not much to look at now, but it will definitely help not having to cart off every case we have to the city to be taken care of."

"Is that what you do now?" Nova asked, curious how it

worked. She'd never expected to be hired by *the* McLintoc Miller Ranch, and she also had absolutely zero experience with how things went at such an automated enterprise. It wasn't like a mom and pop farmer who needed help with their prize cow, or even some of the humane-focused ranches she'd read about up north. Almost everything was done by machine or by contracting it out, so she wasn't sure, with her being an uncertified vet tech, what she was supposed to help with.

However, she was more than happy to learn exactly what she could to be helpful.

"Currently, yes. Granted, this won't be the same as a full clinic. For very serious injuries, sickness, or other things, we'll still have to take them to the city, but this building will be a much better way to treat minor injuries, perform preventative exams, and do rehabilitation."

"And is there much rehabilitation going on here?" It was such a big ranch; she could imagine it might be that way. The tour had been going on for twenty minutes, and apparently, she hadn't even seen a quarter of the pertinent layout yet. She was going to need a while to memorize it if she didn't want to get lost every other day.

"Not a lot, but Amaranth is still getting over a pretty bad fall. We're still trying to get more preventive care and improved treatment for some of the animals here. Mr. Miller tends to treat the livestock like a product instead of living beings."

Well, that was a pretty scathing comment. "If that's true, then why do you work here?" Not that Nova knew the woman well, but when Elizabeth had approached her about the job, the lengthy interview process had given the impression that the tall woman was very intense about quality of animal care.

It also was nice to talk to a woman who was just as tall as her. Sure, there had been a fifteen-minute aside about finding shoes in their size, but other than that, Elizabeth had been intense about finding out everything about Nova's attitude towards animals.

"Because some of his sons feel differently, and while it would be easier to just not be here, there won't be much change if I'm not. Which is the whole reason I secured the funding to bring you on. It can't be just me in the animal's lives. I need another set of hands."

"Don't the sons help?"

"Oh, Solomon, Sterling, and Silas do their best, but they're also handling several other parts of the business. Right now, I believe there's a big to-do because Solomon cut off a contract with a company that was abusing labor laws with their workers."

"Yikes. That sounds... stressful."

"To say the least. But you most likely won't have to worry about it. The dad doesn't ever associate with us lowly workers, Simon is abroad, and Sal is just one person. Besides, I think he hates me because he almost always tries to avoid me."

"That's interesting."

"Yes. There are certainly a lot of ins and outs of working on the Miller Ranch, which you'll figure as the days go on. But first, I do have to ask you something honestly."

Nova's eyebrows went up, anticipation rising in her. She knew that tone.

Elizabeth continued, "This is a very physical job. Are you sure that you'll be able to keep up?"

She was, of course, talking about the knee brace that Nova was sporting and the slight limp she had while walking around. "Oh yeah, I'll be fine. I'm finishing up my own PT and doing better than ever. I'll never be speedy, but I can hold my own."

"Are you sure? I don't want you injuring yourself further just for a paycheck. Thanks to the reach the Millers have, I could probably get you a referral elsewhere."

"I really appreciate that, but I'll be fine, I promise. I've been dealing with this since before I hit puberty and through multiple growth spurts."

"Alright then. I trust your judgment of your own health."

Elizabeth was crisp, that was for certain, and maybe even somewhat intimidating, but her manner made Nova feel comfortable being just as frank. Besides, it wasn't like she was one to lie. Her family may have had a lot of opinions about her, but no one could ever say that she wasn't truthful.

"So, as my tech, you'll be helping calm animals, as well as perform general maintenance. A lot of basic checkups and just making sure that none of them are getting destructive with their behavior."

"Has that been a problem in the past?"

"Oh yeah, when I first started working here, a lot of the pigs were chewing at each other's tails, the barriers, and everything that they shouldn't have. There's been a lot of work put in, and we've still so much to do. Did you know that they just started putting nose tags on their calves this last year?"

"Wait, *what*?"

Nova wasn't the most experienced vet tech, and she'd only worked on a few farms, but as far as she knew, that was basic care. Step one of owning livestock.

"Yeah, like I said, we've done a lot of work. But if you're game to try, I'm still game to bring you on."

"Oh, I'm game, alright," Nova said excitedly. "I've always liked a challenge."

"Alright then, let's finish up your tour."

THE REST of the tour took slightly over an hour, at which time Nova's feet were starting to scream. Apparently, there was more to see, but Elizabeth had been called away to deal with... something. Nova hadn't quite caught the details from the garbled walkie-talkie.

Nova didn't mind, however, and tried hard not to wiggle in excitement as Elizabeth quickly escorted her back to the pigpens. She got the impression that the vet was walking slower than she would have liked, but Nova appreciated the consideration. Slow and steady was her mantra, as she always said. Sure, she might take longer to do something, but it would always get done.

"Alright, so take about two hours for your lunch—you can go to the worker's shack I showed you if you want—then come back here. I'll have Solomon or Silas meet you here for onboarding paperwork."

"Do they really all have 'S' names?"

Elizabeth paused in mid-step of her quick exit. "Rich people," she said as an answer, and Nova instantly knew exactly what she meant.

"Wild."

"Anyway, once you finish your onboarding paperwork, feel free to head home. You'll be paid for the full day, so don't worry." *Score!* "Have a nice night. I look forward to working with you."

"And I look forward to working with you."

Elizabeth gave a nod then hopped into a golf cart beside the pens, racing off as much as a golf cart could. Nova watched her leave and waited until her boss was out of sight before throwing both of her hands in the air and letting out a squeal.

Yes!

Life definitely hadn't been easy for Nova lately, and landing a job as a vet tech that paid *very* well was basically going to change everything. She had been so sure that she was going to have to tuck tail and go back home to her family in the UK that she could hardly believe she had landed the gig.

Good luck was definitely not something she normally had. And the fact that her boss was a black woman in a male-dominated field? Bonus.

Once she was done squealing, she turned around to lean against the pens and look out at her new kingdom—metaphorically speaking, of course. A large sow came trotting up to her, Peggy if Nova remembered correctly.

"Hey there, big lady. Come to officially greet me?" Nova laughed, pressing her leg to the slats of the fence so the pig could sniff at her. She knew better than to stick her hand right in front of an animal that wasn't acquainted with her yet.

But Peggy just sniffed for a moment then honked several times, talking up a storm. Nova listened, thoroughly amused. Elizabeth had said that Peggy was a character—actually, the word she used was *diva*—but it was fun to see that character on full display so soon.

"Is that so?" she asked, chuckling at the very vocal creature. "Tell me more. Tell me all the gossip."

Peggy grunted then proceeded to launch into another long series of snorts, squeals, and sounds. It was pretty entertaining, and Nova was so enthused that she almost missed a slithering streak go right by her foot.

But she *didn't* miss it, and her head snapped in the direction of the movement.

Was that a *mud snake*? Nova hadn't seen one of those in a while.

"You hold that thought, Peggy," Nova said, turning away and following after. She should probably leave the thing alone, but it was by a place where it was pretty easy to get trampled or hurt by a worker. Maybe even eaten up by a pig. And while Nova believed in the circle of life and all that; she also really, *really* loved reptiles.

Besides, it was her lunchtime. If she wanted to spend it following a snake, who was to stop her?

Hurrying along as best she could, she kept her eyes on the black and red snake as it scuttled along. They were nonvenomous, and probably great for helping to keep the mouse population down, but it would do better maybe away from the parking area and more towards the fields. And hey, if it changed directions and went to safety, she figured that she could just enjoy watching it shimmy along.

The whole demi-chase was going great until she lost it somewhere around the back of the barn. One moment it was there, the next it was just... gone.

Huh, that was disappointing.

Oh well, it wasn't like she was going to pick it up and keep it. It didn't look injured, and there was no reason it needed to be helped. But still... didn't mean she couldn't maybe possibly hold it for a solid thirty seconds or so.

Nova turned in place a moment, hands on her hips. She was pretty sure the lil' guy was long gone, but she figured walking once around the barn wouldn't hurt.

Taking her time, she ambled along, looking for him all curled up in some corner. She was maybe halfway around when she heard a yelp. A yelp that distinctly sounded like a non-snake-liking person coming face to face with a snake. As someone who loved reptiles, it was something she was used to hearing more often than she liked.

Rushing around as best she could with her bum knee, she came right around a corner of the barn to see a truly giant man with a shovel raised above his head, the mud snake cornered between two pieces of equipment and desperately trying to find an escape.

"Hey! Stop that!" she cried. There was no reason to kill an innocent, non-venomous creature that actually helped the ecosystem of the ranch. Maybe it was crazy of her to object, considering how some people felt about them, but just because they freaked some people out was no reason to *murder* one.

But the man's bulging arms—seriously, he had a *lot* of muscle—were already coming down. He wasn't going to stop.

A problem that Nova had occasionally was that her logic sometimes came second to her emotions. It was something that her family had complained about since she was a kid, but it hadn't changed even into her adulthood.

And that was how she ended up charging forward and tackling a guy with at least eighty pounds on her.

Well, her mother had always said she had more heart than head. And that was the last thought that popped into her head right before she crashed into a solid wall of muscle.

Umph.

3

Salvatore

*S*al was having a very strange day.

One minute, he was standing there, about to kill a snake that he'd just cornered, the next it felt like someone threw a bale of hay at him, hitting him right in the side.

He hadn't exactly been expecting to be tackled while going about his day on the ranch, so he stumbled, his foot slipping on the loose gravel around the western side of the barn. The next thing he knew, he was falling to his knees and the shovel in his hand was bouncing off somewhere else.

What was going on?

A groan sounded from in front of him, shaking him from the surprise of the situation, and he realized that there was a woman splayed out on the ground in front of him, her face twisted in a grimace.

"What on earth did you do that for?" he snapped, not even

getting up on his feet yet. He was too sideswiped by the entire situation. Had someone really just *assaulted* him on his own ranch?

"What do you mean, what on earth was that for?" she snapped back, working her way to sitting up. She was taller than he expected, their heights much closer even with her on her *tuchus*. And she was glaring at him like *he* was the one running around tackling people, her dark brown eyes using far stronger language than her mouth was. "You were going to kill a snake."

"*Yeah,*" he retorted like it was the most obvious thing on earth, because it was. The woman in front of him had to be insane. "Because it's a dangerous animal!"

"Mud snakes are harmless and help reduce the amount of vermin that can become a problem in a farm setting," she snapped back. "Just because you don't like something doesn't mean it's dangerous."

He got to his feet, glaring down at the woman, but the impact of the stare was lessened when she started to rise too. Granted, she swayed slightly, pinwheeling her arms to catch her balance, and that was when he noticed the brace on her leg.

She had an injury and had still crashed into him that hard? That didn't seem possible.

But then she was finally all the way up so he could get his first good look at her, and suddenly the force of her tackle made sense.

The woman was tall, at least as tall as Elizabeth, but instead of being lean and muscled like the veterinarian, she was softer. Sal wasn't exactly the most hip to pop culture, but she was bottom-heavy in a way that he was pretty sure was popular with certain celebrities. Her shoulders were broad, but not disproportionately so, and she had a distinctive sort of bone structure that he wasn't used to seeing.

"There's no way you knew what kind of snake that was."

"What are you talking about? Glossy black underside combined with a red and black topside with a reddish-pink blend along the sides? Then you add that it clearly didn't have any preocular scales with only one internasal scale, and that's a mud snake if I've ever seen one." The woman huffed.

"I... *what*?" Those were certainly words that she had used, but he didn't know what any of them meant. What about scales? "There's no way you saw that."

"Why, just because you can't?" Her hands were on her wide hips, and she was affixing him a *look*. It didn't help that her dark brown hair was kept into a stylish sort of pixie cut, so there wasn't even bangs or a shadow to lessen the intensity of that glower.

Sal was abruptly very done with the conversation. She had *no* right to talk to him like that. Although she was dressed as a civilian, she had to be an employee. Unless one of his brothers had suddenly taken on another girlfriend. Granted, considering how crazy they were acting, maybe that was a possibility.

"Yeah, unfortunately, running this ranch as a Miller doesn't exactly leave room for extracurricular studies about random farm snakes."

There it was. She would realize who he was and start backpedaling, asking for forgiveness. Which he *definitely* wasn't going to do with all her attitude. In fact, she would be lucky if he didn't sue her right then and there.

"Maybe if you're going to run a ranch, you should be educated about the type of animals that are beneficial to it."

She didn't even blink. *What*?

That wasn't how it was supposed to work. Her eyes were

supposed to go wide, her cheeks were supposed to flush, and then the apologies were supposed to come pouring out.

What was the world coming to? He was basically her employer! Where was the respect? The deference? His family was the one that put food on her family's table, and she was mouthing off to him like they were on equal footing.

It was just like Dad said, the younger generation had no respect for anything. Always *me, me, me,* and never caring about anything outside themselves. That was why they wanted to bail on their loans and were always demanding handouts.

He took a deep breath, not sure what he was going to say but knowing it would be absolutely *scathing,* when suddenly there was a shout and someone coming around the corner.

"What's going on here? Was someone hurt?"

He wasn't pleased to see it was Elizabeth, her expression serious as usual. Did that woman *ever* smile on the clock, or did she charge for that?

"You know this worker?" Sal heard himself bark. Usually he knew better than to use any sort of tone like that with the vet because she would get *real* icy, but his temper was sparking so high, so fast, that he couldn't keep the bite out of it.

Besides, he shouldn't *have* to! They were both *his* employees!

"That's my assistant you're talking to," Elizabeth said flatly, her eyes flicking between the two of them. "The vet tech that was approved in the last budget report."

Ah, Sal remembered that particular conversation. It had been a three-hour fight between Dad and the twins, if only because it wasn't *just* a vet tech that his brothers wanted. No, it was also a huge expansion in addition to all the money that they were already hemorrhaging for their bleeding-heart animal care.

"*Ex*-assistant," he snapped. "She needs to be fired. *Immediately.*"

A sputter sounded from the woman beside him, but it was more of an enraged noise than the placating one that he expected. Wasn't she going to even try to *beg* for her job?

"Fire her? What exactly happened here?"

"She laid hands on me."

"He was trying to kill a snake for no reason! It wasn't even dangerous!"

They spoke at the same time and their words were mostly a jumble, but Elizabeth seemed to understand them well enough. Her eyes flashed, and then she was crossing her arms, face stony.

"Nova, you come with me. Have a good day, Sal."

"What?" he asked, his temper spiking yet again. "She tackled me. Fire her, immediately."

But Elizabeth wasn't even looking at him, already turning away. "Take it up with your brothers if you're that concerned," she said without an ounce of caring to her tone.

The woman, Nova, apparently—what kind of name was *Nova*, anyway?—rushed to follow after her. The two disappeared around the barn.

What on earth was going on!?

Sal was standing there, fuming, but completely alone. He was a *Miller*. That was supposed to *mean* something. His family worked hard and provided for so many people. Where was the gratitude?

Nowhere, apparently.

Well, Elizabeth said to talk to his brother, so he stormed back to the house to do just that.

4

Nova

*N*ova was going to be fired.

She was sure of it. She couldn't believe that she had tackled one of the sons of the ranching empire she worked for on her very first day. Who did that? Her, apparently. And all over a snake.

Actually, she wasn't upset about that last part. Shovels weren't exactly precise killing instruments, and chances were that the snake would be grievously injured, not ended outright, and it would slick away to die some agonizing and unnecessarily painful death.

If her mother was there, she would no doubt be chewing Nova's ear off about ruining such an excellent opportunity. She could almost hear it in her head, the diatribe winding around her brain and twisting in her ears. It was like being back home again, which was actually pretty terrible.

At least Elizabeth hadn't dressed her down right in front of the fuming Miller son. Because *man*, that guy was big and maybe also a little scary. Nova didn't know if she'd ever met anyone whose biceps were literally the size of her head, but that lad was built like a comic book superhero.

Actually... he was pretty handsome like one too. She hadn't paid any attention to it at first, but as she replayed the situation over and over again in her mind, she remembered more of his face than she had in the moment.

And it was a *nice* face.

Some muscular guys ended up looking kinda froggy, but there was nothing amphibian about the giant man. He'd had a classically square jaw that blended exceptionally well into his prominent cheekbones and curly, sandy blond hair, which made his green eyes stand out that much more. He might have been a model, if he hadn't looked so rugged, stubble about his cheeks and eyebrows that needed more grooming if there were photoshoots involved.

But he definitely wasn't a model, because of course, he was her boss's boss. Talk about needing to look before she leaped. Yet another situation she had ruined because of dumb luck.

Well, dumb luck and an ardent love of reptiles. It wasn't *their* fault that people thought they were creepy. That was just how God made them.

Elizabeth basically burst into the barn, startling the couple of workers who were there. Nova could practically feel the look she gave them as the vet cleared her throat.

"Could we have a few minutes, please?"

Well, at least if she was about to read Nova the riot act, she was choosing to do it in private. Nova was grateful for the small things in life.

But when the place was cleared and Elizabeth finally

turned to her, there was no shouting. There was no reprimand even. Instead, the woman's face split into a wide grin before she busted out laughing.

Oh.

She was... not mad?

Something wasn't computing, but Nova waited a good two to three minutes for the vet's peals of mirth to calm down. It wasn't until the woman was trying to catch her breath and wiping tears from her eyes that Nova had the gumption to speak up.

"Is everything okay?" she asked finally.

"Okay? Is everything okay?" Elizabeth repeated, clapping and getting lost in another minute or so of laughing. "Are you kidding me? I thought I was going to *die* out there from trying to hold this in. Did you see Sal's face? Kid looked redder than the sun!" Another chuckle, a cough, and then another chuckle. "You'll have to excuse me, but Salvatore Miller has been giving me the stink eye ever since we met, and it was *so* nice to see him completely off-balance."

Nova wasn't sure what strange world she had woken up in, but she was pretty sure her terrible luck somehow wasn't getting worse. "So... I'm not fired then?"

That seemed to sober Elizabeth up. "Fired? What? No! Why would you be fired?"

"I, uh, I basically hit one of the owners of the ranch. Seems like it would be a big deal."

But Elizabeth just waved her hand as if it didn't matter. "You stopped someone who was going to make a harmful mistake in the most expedient way you could. If worse comes to worst, I'll have you apologize to him for the startle, but he's a big boy. He can handle a little shove." She snorted again and *man,* if that wasn't just about the last sound that she expected to hear from Elizabeth. "I can't believe you got that giant onto the ground. He is a *big* boy."

"Yeah, really is amazing, isn't it?" Nova said with her own half-laugh. She was still in shock from what she had done and clearly not nearly as amused as Elizabeth was.

"Yup. I cannot wait to tell Sterling about this. Let me check the time." She pulled her phone out and frowned. "Oh, I thought we were past lunch. He's probably still asleep."

"He a late riser?"

"Kind of," she said with a shrug. "He has trouble sleeping more than four hours at a time, so he usually passes out around ten, wakes up at two, then putters around until six or seven and sleeps until noon-adjacent. He's always up and dressed in time for our lunch dates, of course."

"Lunch dates?" Nova repeated, the switch in the conversation making her head do a one-eighty.

"Oh right, Sterling and I are dating. It's a long story, just know that it doesn't conflict with the job in any way, and you shouldn't expect any special treatment." Her full lips quirked into a smile. "Well, special treatment beyond getting away with shoving a billionaire around."

Another nervous laugh from Nova. "Good to know." But there was that nagging feeling inside of her that it couldn't be that easy. "Are you sure that we won't get into trouble?"

"We'll be fine. If you were stealing, hurting the animals, or purposefully harming anyone here, I'd have you out the door faster than you could say the Lord's prayer. But that's not the case, so you don't have anything to worry about. Although..." The vet seemed to consider something, and Nova's heart jumped. She *knew* it was too good to be true. "You know what, maybe you should lay low for a tiny bit. Why don't you head home for the rest of the day? Full pay, of course."

"Uh, sure. If you don't think I should do the onboarding stuff..."

"Well, ideally you would, but I'm pretty sure there's about to be a fight at the big house, so Solomon probably won't be free to do much of anything but deal with his brother. I'm sure that will all blow over by tomorrow, and we can get the paperwork done then."

"Alright then. I'll bring my tax information tomorrow too."

"Oh! And before you go, hold on, I have something for you." She reached into her pocket then offered Nova up a business card. "This is a mechanic I know in the city. She's great and worked on my own car. Have her look at your junker, since it's a long drive back and forth."

"Oh, uh, okay." Nova took it, looking down at the clean and simple card. *Andre's Mechanic Service.* Huh. Andre didn't sound like a woman's name.

"Alright, well, since that's all taken care of, let me escort you to your car so you can get home and digest everything that just happened. Because, lemme tell you, this is probably the most exciting first day of work that I've experienced in a long while. Whoo, I can't wait to tell my dad about this, he'll get a real kick out of it."

"Glad that I could be entertaining."

"Better than being boring."

"Right, so—" the vet stopped short. "Nova, are you aware that your shirt is wiggling?"

"What? Oh. Right." Pulling her shirt away from her body, she carefully pulled the mud snake out from under her shirt. It was *not* happy, but she bent down and let it wiggle out of her hand to disappear across the floor. There were enough exits and hidey-holes that she wasn't overly worried about it being bothered.

"You're kidding me," Elizabeth said, laughing again. "We're gonna get along just fine."

Nova sensed that there was a story there, but she didn't ask. Instead, she just nodded along as they walked back to her car. Elizabeth seemed as happy as a clam, but Nova's stomach was twisting with nerves. She almost felt like Salvatore was going to pop out at any moment, but thankfully he didn't, and soon she was on the road.

Elizabeth was right about it being a long drive. Nova had been leery about the job at first for that very reason, but then the *pay* had been real convincing. And it wasn't like she was going to be bored. She had podcasts on her phone, plenty of music as well as a language learning app for German and French. And naturally a car charger to make sure her old-as-dirt phone didn't die. She knew she should get a newer smartphone, but it was just so *expensive*. Her battery lasted about a solid two hours before needing to be charged or connected to an external battery, but she made do.

In fact, she was only a quarter through her driving playlist when she pulled up to her apartment complex. Sure, it wasn't the nicest place, but it was cheap, and she managed to land a pretty okay studio apartment. Sure, it only had a shower, and sure, there was barely enough room for her hips in the tiny kitchenette, but there was no mold, no critters, and they only asked for a half a security deposit plus rent.

Putting her important documents into the glove compartment, she headed up the stairs to her place. She wasn't a huge fan of the number of steps between the ground floor and her front door, but it wasn't like she could exactly complain. Especially since it was her first time not living in a room for rent since she'd moved out on her own.

Besides, with the money she was making, once her six-month lease was over, she was pretty sure that she could move up to a one-bedroom apartment. Then she would *really* have lots of space and maybe be able to get some more house plants to liven the place up.

Lost to her daydreams, Nova went to her kitchen for the lunch that she didn't get to have thanks to her going all front-end tackle on a rich bodybuilder. It'd been a couple of weeks since she'd had a solid paycheck—her retail job having cut her hours when one of her coworkers ratted on her for looking for a new job-—so her choices were instant ramen, mac n' cheese, toast or rice.

Shrugging to herself, she set up her rice cooker and pulled some left-over soy sauce packets from when she'd gone to a friend's party and they'd all ordered Chinese. That was the great thing about rice, considering that she had hot sauce, duck sauce, soy sauce and cheese, she could really mix it up into a lot of flavor profiles and keep it fresh. That was one of the keys to inexpensive living, learning how to make low-cost food not boring. Goodness knew she had plenty of experience.

Once her rice was all set up to cook, she went to her couch and flopped there, kicking off her shoes over the armrest. Once she was comfortable, she pulled her laptop up and opened up the transcribing program she used to make money on the side. It wasn't very lucrative or easy, but it kept her housed and fed even in the unpredictable world of a rotating retail schedule.

Settling down for the night, she got to work, feeling more hopeful about her future than she had in a long while.

5

Salvatore

*S*al didn't actually have a plan of how he was going to confront his brothers, what he was going to say, or even which brother he should talk to. And in retrospect, that was probably his first mistake in his furious march back to the main house.

He should have known better. Given that it was noon, that usually meant that Solomon was in his office or in the city with that French girl and Silas was doing some sort of dumb manual repair somewhere, so that meant the only brother he even *could* find would be Sterling, fresh up from his second sleep and most likely rooting around in the kitchen for a dorky picnic lunch to take to his irritating girlfriend.

And sure enough, as Sal stormed into the house, he caught sight of Sterling bent half into the fridge, rummaging around for food. It irked Sal that Elizabeth was not only being paid well over the market average, but she also was constantly being fed from their kitchen. In fact, all of the ladies ate from their kitchen fairly often. He thought that they'd be more grateful considering all that was provided to them courtesy of the Miller family, but *nooo*, they were evil corporate overlords.

Sal rolled his eyes and went straight to his brother, clearing his throat when he was just behind the younger twin. Sterling jumped, whirling around with a shout.

"Whoa, Sal, some personal space, would ya? You startled me."

But Sal didn't even bother with a reply, going straight into his diatribe.

"You need to get control of your woman and have her fire that girl she just hired."

"What are you talking about?"

Sterling blinked at him, like Salvatore was speaking another language, and that just made Sal's irritation rise that much further.

"I said—"

"No, I know what you said, I was just giving you a chance to turn that sentence around if you wanted me to actually give a red cent about what you're saying." Sterling shook his head, a dismissive expression crossing his face.

That was the opposite of what Sal had wanted, which of course made his temper burn that much hotter. He worked so hard; why did none of his brothers respect him?

Sterling continued, "My woman? Really? You're lucky Elizabeth's not around to hear you call her that because I don't think I'd be able to stop her from laying you out."

Sal felt his chest swell. As if she *could*. "That's the thing! Her employee, that girl she hired, tackled me!"

"Wait, the new tech? The one with an accent and a knee brace?"

Wait, she'd had an accent? Sal had been so blindsided, so caught up in his anger that he hadn't even noticed. "Yes, the one with a leg brace! How many techs is she hiring?!"

"Whoa, you need to take it down about three notches, brother. You've got, what, a hundred pounds on that girl. I'm sure you're fine."

Sal couldn't believe it. "It's not about being fine! It's about respect to the company—"

"What were you doing?"

"Pardon?"

"Look, you're a mountain of muscle and bigger than all of the rest of us. A young lady in a knee brace isn't just going to dive tackle you for no reason. What happened? Did you scare her? You two just run into each other around a corner?"

"*No*, we did not just run into each other around a corner. I was about to kill a snake when she completely blindsided me and I slid on the gravel! I had a shovel; we both could have been hurt!"

"Wait, why were you trying to kill a snake?"

"Because snakes are *dangerous*. They kill chickens and scare horses and—"

"Did it look like a copperhead or a rattlesnake?"

Sal just blinked at his brother right back. The conversation was *not* going how he had envisioned it. "No, it wasn't a rattlesnake and I don't remember how a copperhead looks."

"Huh, maybe you should look that up then. Some of the snakes around here are actually pretty good for the ranch's ecosystems. They keep the rat population down, but also end up being food for some of the wild birds who also keep the rat population down. All in all, better to not go around killin' animals for just being animals."

"Are you being serious right now?"

"Yeah, Sal. I mean, did the snake rattle at you? Or hiss? Or even strike? Or was it trying to run away... "

"I... I don't know. I just saw it and reacted."

"Look, I know you spend most of your time inside or working on the more person-to-person parts of the business, but maybe it would help you to familiarize yourself with the native critters around here. Anyway, I'm gonna be late to lunch if I don't hurry."

"So you're not gonna fire the girl? Even though she laid hands on your brother?"

"No, I don't think I'm too keen on firing anybody, Sal. Especially if she was just stopping one of us from making a mistake."

Sal could feel the shaking starting up his arms, something that always happened when his temper was getting too riled up too quickly. When he was younger, he would have slugged his brother for making him so mad, but he knew better now.

He was far too strong to just punch someone willy-nilly, even if he was angry. And if he wasn't responsible enough to keep his muscles in check, then he didn't deserve them.

Taking a deep breath, he turned on his heel and stalked out. If his brothers wouldn't see reason, he'd go straight to his dad and rat them out.

...maybe after a shower and some deep breathing.

Turned out that he needed a *lot* of deep breathing, ending up meditating for nearly thirty minutes before he felt like he was ready to go inform his father in a cool, confident manner. Striding to his parents' wing, he went to his father's study and knocked on the door.

He figured it was hit or miss to the man actually being around. Considering that last election season hadn't gone in his father's favor, McLintoc Miller had been taking to golfing with his buddies and doing more "war room" sessions to gear up for the next round. Personally, Sal didn't get the obsession with winning office, but that was why he wasn't the brains of the business.

Or at least that was what his father always liked to tell him. Sal certainly didn't appreciate those comments, but there was a reason Solomon had been chosen to be the heir to the company and not Sal.

Then again... things were changing. If Sal proved himself, maybe he would have a chance at the top spot and his brothers would stop treating him like a muscle-headed afterthought.

Fat chance.

"What is it?"

"Hey, Dad," Sal said, opening the door and letting himself in. McLintoc Miller was in his favorite chair, reading another biography about some rich dead guy. Sal had learned to stop asking which dead guy, as usually all the stories ended up pretty much the same. And Sal actually *liked* reading, despite what people assumed about him. "I wanted to bring up a personal issue with the new hire from the last budget discussion we had."

"Are you kidding me right now?"

Sal couldn't help but be surprised at his dad's sudden response. It was laced with both vehemence and irritation, and Sal couldn't think of what he had done to earn such ire right off the bat.

"Um... no?"

"*Son,*" his dad said, closing his book and giving him the most admonishing look Sal had been on the receiving end of in quite a long time. "I am dealing with an all-out coup from your brothers and our board. Serious stuff involving the future of our business. There's so much to be worried about with those three determined to upend everything that I've worked to build that I don't have the time or the patience to hear about whatever little squabble you've had now.

"For Pete's sake, you're twenty-six now, Salvatore. Man up. I can't keep holding your hand like you're a child. Even Simon is out doing things of his own volition, even if they are a waste of time."

Sal swallowed, a deluge of reactions rushing through him. He was the biggest of the Miller sons, but why did his father always make him feel so small? Like he was still that skinny, high school runt who everyone said didn't even look like a Miller. It wasn't a good feeling, and he just so desperately wanted his father to be proud of him. Why was that too much to ask?

"I'm sorry," he ground out, all of his anger deflating. This was why he wasn't the heir of the empire. He was too dumb, too childish. "What can I do to help? I want to be useful."

Dad sighed, rolling his eyes before sitting up. "Fine, if you really need me to hold your hand. What you need to do is establish dominance and stop acting like such a pushover. Win over at least some of the workers because they all seem to be drooling after Solomon's new benefit package and the twin's obsession with updating all of our perfectly fine equipment.

"Show them that they don't need all that stuff, and in the end the more *we* make, the more job security they have. In the long run, your brother's plans will leave them with less than they have now rather than more."

Sal wasn't exactly sure how that worked out, but he wasn't going to argue.

His dad continued, "After all, we're not socialists. We're true-blue Americans, and we work hard for our country and freedom."

"Right. Of course. I will do that, and I'll keep at it until it works. Failure is not an option."

"You've got that right."

Nodding, Sal excused himself and headed back out, but as the door to his dad's study closed, he couldn't help but feel entirely exhausted. Except exhausted didn't seem to do his mood justice. Worn. Inside out. Deflated.

Well, whatever the right phrase was, he was pretty sure that he could use a nap. And then a workout. Nothing like a session in his personal gym to forget his worries.

He certainly had plenty.

IT TOOK Sal about two days to gather himself and figure out the start of his plan. He figured the best place to begin was to confront Silas or Solomon and tell them that they needed to shape up. After all, there was a chance that they were just so punch-drunk from their lady friends that they weren't thinking straight. Maybe, if he was concise and direct, he could shed some light for them, and their family could go back to being a family instead of two conflicting factions.

He could always hope.

Stealing himself, he headed up to Solomon's office. Normally he didn't make a habit of going over to his brother's wing, but he figured uniting his family was a pretty good cause. Of course, when he got there and knocked on the door, it became clear pretty quickly that he wasn't in.

He had to be off to the city again. Drat. It seemed like he

spent more time there than home lately. That certainly wasn't helping.

Oh well, there was always Silas. Chances were he was just going off to his morning ride. And if that failed, well, Sterling would be up in a few hours.

Nodding to himself, Sal headed out the door. Silas' truck was still in their extended garage, so that bode well, but he had no idea where his brother was on the ranch. He supposed he could text the elder twin, but he didn't want the forewarning, giving his brother a chance to make up some sort of excuse as to why they couldn't meet.

Well, if his brother was out on a ride, he had to return to the stables eventually. Especially since he wasn't riding on his favorite horse, Amaranth, as she was still recovering from her injury last summer.

Feeling pleased to have a plan, Sal grabbed one of their spare golf carts and headed towards the stables. He'd been skeptical when Solomon had suggested the little things as a way to cut down on their emissions in riding around the ranch, but the carts turned out to be pretty fun. Besides, Sal saw how much his mother had giggled when she'd first gotten her flowery one and, well, if it made his momma happy, he was alright with it.

It took longer to get there than it would in a truck, of course, but he wasn't in a hurry. For the past year and a half, Silas had taken to horseback riding in the morning, racing his twin or just exploring around the ranch. Sal didn't entirely get it, but he didn't begrudge his brother in enjoying the horses. They were magnificent creatures.

When he arrived, he heard noises inside that indicated a human was in there along with all the mounts. Perfect.

Striding in, he was all ready to confront his brother only to see that it wasn't Silas at all.

No, instead it was the last person he ever wanted to see. Just his luck.

It was the crazy girl, the one who had tackled him, mucking out a stall and humming to herself with her earbuds in. She gave no indication that she even noticed him standing there and that irritated Sal for some reason.

Striding over, he cleared his throat once, twice, then a third time while rapping on the stall's partition before she jumped, yanking her headphones from her ears.

"Jeeza-Louise! You really move silently for a hench chap, don't you?" she exclaimed, hand over her chest.

Her accent and slang startled him, and he found his eyes automatically scanning her over again to catch anything he missed after their rather tumultuous first meeting. She wasn't wearing the usual button-up and khakis that Elizabeth sported, or the jumpsuit that other workers wore. Instead she was wearing a sort of fitted gray tank that looked like it might have once been white, and thick black leggings. It was a skin-tight outfit, and he found his eyes being drawn appreciatively to places where it wasn't polite to stare, and that irritated him too.

"Is that how you always greet your employer?" he reiterated. Sure, she hadn't exactly been humble the last time that they had interacted, but that was back when emotions and adrenaline had been running high. Maybe after some time simmering in what she had done, she would be more gracious.

"No, but it is usually how I react when someone scares me half to death. What are you, some sort of ninja-cowboy hybrid?"

His eyebrows furrowed more than he meant for them to. "I'm not a cowboy."

"You literally own a ranch."

"Yes. Because I'm a rancher."

"Eh, six in one hand, half dozen in the other. You deal with cows, then you're a cowboy, wouldn't you say mate?"

Sal could feel himself bristling. He didn't like how the woman seemed so completely unruffled by him. Normally people were intimidated by his stature, charmed by his looks, or interested in his money. But the woman in front of him was acting like he was just some nobody from the street. And while Sal was a lot of things, a *nobody* wasn't one of them.

"And as a British person, you're obviously the expert on what makes a cowboy or not."

"Exactly, now you're getting it." She laughed cheerily, as if they were friends. They were most definitely *not* friends. "Anyway, what can I do you for? Did Elizabeth need something?"

"I wouldn't know. I don't run errands for Elizabeth."

"Oh, then what do you do?"

Her tone was polite as punch and the look she had on her face was earnest. *Too* earnest. She was playing him. She was playing him and they both knew it. Frustration prickled up his spine and spilled onto his tongue, making it stick to the roof of his mouth. He hadn't counted on the woman who tackled him being *clever*. Physical violence and a smart mouth usually didn't go hand in hand.

Why was he even wasting time talking to her? It wasn't like she was worth his time. Like Dad had said, he needed to concentrate on things that were actually important to the business.

"Nothing you need to know about," he said curtly before

turning away. It was the last word alright, but a hollow victory and he knew as much. Oh well.

However, he only managed to get maybe a single step away before a sharp click sounded behind him, almost like someone snapping two tines of a pitchfork against each other. Then there was a gasp, a curse, a thump, and then a noise that definitely was a tool falling.

Spinning back around, Sal wasn't sure what to expect, but it certainly wasn't the girl sitting square on her butt right in the middle of the empty stall.

"What just happened?" he asked gruffly, trying to see if something had knocked her over or she'd been kicked by a horse from another stall somehow.

"Ah, I turned wrong," she said with a wince. "I'm pretty sure I dislocated my knee."

Alarm bells went off in Sal's head. People didn't just dislocate their knees from turning. Instantly his mind went to insurance fraud, and suddenly all of the woman's bizarre actions and bold attitude made sense.

He opened his mouth to tell her that he wasn't going to fall for her scheme, but before he got a single syllable out, the woman was rolling up her pants and then gripping either side of her knee.

Oh... it did look *real* funny, bulging in the wrong spot. That wasn't good.

He barely had time to lean forward for a better look when the girl jerked her hands in a particular way and a resounding *CRACK* filled the barn, startling several of the horses.

Had she just...

She didn't just...

No. That did *not* happen.

"There we go," she said with a relieved sort of breath as she shakily got back to her feet. Sal stared openly, noticing how the joint was flushed an angry red but not bulging in that very weird way anymore.

"I..." Sal started before swallowing. He couldn't believe that he had just watched a woman pop her dislocated knee back into position like it wasn't an issue. Surely that wasn't normal. "Do you need me to call you a doctor?"

She let out a snort. "Please! Like I'm gonna pay someone a couple of hundred dollars to give my knee a jerk. I've done it plenty of times myself, so I know what I'm doing." She started doing some gentle stretches, like she was warming up for a run rather than just having done a medical procedure on herself in the middle of a horse stall. "Besides, I really wanted to get this done before Silas came back from his ride. As sort of a thank-you for the walk-through he's going to give me with Amaranth and Obelisk."

Sal continued to stare at her like she was a three-headed dragon as she slowly worked her leg up and down, then bent it gingerly. After a few moments, she seemed satisfied and went back to muckraking like nothing had happened at all.

What on *earth?*

Clearly, he had been dismissed, nonverbally at that. He lingered a moment, not entirely sure that he was in the real world, but eventually he drifted off, his head spinning. Were all British women so particular, or was she a special case?

He didn't know, but it was making more sense why a woman who could casually pop her own joints in an out of place without even flinching had no problem tackling him. He didn't know when the world had turned upside down, but she was one to watch out for.

6

Nova

*J*ust three more.
    Two more.
    One more good one...
Aaaand done!

Nova practically collapsed back on the mat, sweating like a horse and feeling like a limp noodle that had been cooked long past overdone. It wasn't unusual for her physical therapy to be a challenge, but her therapist had decided to put her through the wringer that day.

It was apparently to deal with the inflammation around her knee since she had dislocated it again. It had been a couple months since she had done that, but she wasn't too alarmed.

Ever since her doctors back on the base had made her walk on a shattered knee for about a year, she'd always had issues. It grated against itself, popped in and out, and generally did what it wanted. Nova didn't know why her knee couldn't want to do something *convenient* for her, but she guessed it had a right to be upset since she spent twelve whole months straight up abusing it during her formative years. It didn't help that she had an insane growth spurt and ended up being a dash over six-foot tall.

"Goodness, you're so strong. Are you sure you need to even be here?"

Nova turned her head at the friendly comment, seeing an older woman standing just off the mat. She was dressed in the typical outfit one might expect from a senior citizen at physical therapy, her white hair done up in a sensible bun and her wrinkled cheeks flushed.

"Thanks," Nova said politely. She was so exhausted; she didn't really have it in her to have a full-blown conversation. She hoped that the woman would be happy with a short-but-sweet response and then be on her way.

"What are you here for? Clearly your arms and shoulders are in tip-top shape! I remember when I was young and strong."

Nova really, *really* believed in respecting her elders, but she was just so *tired*, and the warm sweat she'd worked up was quickly cooling into something damp and uncomfortable. She wasn't nearly in the right mood to have a conversation with a stranger, but she didn't feel like she could ignore the woman either.

"Thank you, I stay active."

The woman lingered again, and Nova felt a roil of awkwardness go right up her back. Ugh. She tried to think of what to say, a polite term that said, "I appreciate you and your time, but I'm too exhausted to socialize right now," but nothing came to her.

"Well, I'm off to do the cardio the therapist keeps harping at me about. You have a lovely day, young lady."

"You too. Be safe."

The older woman looked from Nova then to the equipment over on the other side of the facility, then back before tottering off, leaving Nova to her heavy panting.

She knew she needed to get up before she got stiff, so with a groan, Nova got to her feet. Well... got to her butt first, took a few deep breaths and thought about where she was in the world and just exactly how the force of gravity felt on every joint of her body, then she pushed herself up to her feet and wobbled around the mat until she felt like she could walk a straight line.

Part of her wanted to just say goodbye and walk out of the door, but she knew that there were at least three more exercises that she was supposed to do before he came back. So she headed over to the strange sort of circle platform with half of an exercise ball in the center of it, stood on that little bump and tried to balance while doing her leg lifts.

So *many* leg lifts.

It was about another half hour before Nova wobbled over to where her PT was refilling his bottle. When she had first started, he'd been with her during every moment of every exercise, but thankfully they'd built up enough trust in each other to let Nova go some of the simpler ones on her own.

"Hey there, you look worked out."

"That's because I am," Nova said with a laugh, leaning against the wall. "Am I clear to go?"

"I'm not quite sure. I'm worried about that knee of yours

dislocating after so long. And you said that it just happened, there wasn't an injury? Or fall?"

"Well, I may have tackled someone a few days earlier, and we both fell."

True to character, her physical therapist's eyebrows shot up. "You tackled someone?"

"Uh-huh."

"Any reason?"

"I was saving a snake."

"Ah, of course. And this person, they didn't happen to be smaller than you, maybe a child or otherwise very soft human?"

"Nope, guy was six foot five and built like a brick house."

"Right. Well. So that definitely could have exacerbated this issue. Your muscles are still pretty inflamed, and I'm worried about them locking up or building up scar tissue even worse, so I'm going to show you some exercises you can do at home. I want you to do them every day."

"And then I can go home?"

He crooked a smile at her, his brows pushing into a faux-upset look. "What, you saying that you don't like hanging out with me?"

"Well, you are kinda a pain in my butt. And everywhere else, for that matter."

"Yeah, but that's my job. It's literally what you pay me for."

"I suppose it is, isn't it?"

They shared a laugh and walked over to the equipment and mat area, where he walked Nova through the exercises. She worked hard, and when she was done, Nova really *did* feel like a limp noodle.

From there it was a hurried goodbye and a drive back to her place so she could shower. She took her time, staying in until the hot water was all gone and enjoying every minute of it. Once she was out, she dried herself off, got into comfy clothes, and then headed over to collapse onto her couch and veg out.

Of course, the moment her butt touched the cushion, an urgent buzzing sounded from her phone. Someone was calling her? No one ever *called* her anymore. Most of her friends were back in the UK, and they always texted each other first to make sure that the other party was awake.

Flipping her phone over, she saw that it was Elizabeth calling her.

What could she want?

"Hello?" Nova asked, sitting up like the vet could see her.

"Hey, what are you up to? Are you busy?"

"No, just got home, actually. Why?"

"I've got a cow here that's having some trouble, and I'm going to step in on the birth in an hour or two. There's no better way to learn than firsthand, so I was wondering if you wanted to boogie on down? I got approval from Sterling for some overtime."

Oh, man. Nova was *exhausted*, down to her very bones. But Elizabeth was offering a great opportunity, one that didn't exactly come by in droves. Especially considering that it wasn't even birthing season.

"Alright. I'll head out right now. Be there as soon as I can. I did just get out of PT, so I'm shaky and limpy from the work-out. Nothing I can't handle, though."

"Alright, I trust your judgment. Call me when you're at the drive. Talk to you soon."

"Yeah, talk to you soon."

∼

HELPING BIRTH A CALF WAS *AMAZING*.

Even though Nova mostly just stood beside Elizabeth, handing her things when she needed and gently petting the cow's head, she was *so* glad she had forced herself to get out of the apartment and speed to the ranch. The experience was invaluable, and even if her legs were screaming at her when it was all said and done, it was more than worth it.

Also, it felt good to be *trusted* already. She'd barely been at the job a week and her boss was calling her in for surprise overtime to bring a new life into the world? Amazing. Nova hadn't felt so vital at a job since well... *ever*. And although she knew Elizabeth would have been fine without her help, it just was such a nice change that Nova's efforts provided noticeable relief.

Maybe that was why she was so drawn to animal care in the first place. Her lofty dreams had been to be an actual vet, but considering how expensive and long she would have to go to school for that, it was much too far out of her reach. Especially considering that her grades had only been average growing up. If only scholarships took into account that being constantly made into a villain by her family could really tank a teenager's motivation to do anything.

Nova shook her head as she hobbled to her car, thighs protesting with every single step. She wasn't going to ruin the wonderful feelings in her by thinking about her family. Not when helping Elizabeth had helped her feel so useful and smart. Basically everything they'd told her she wasn't. She'd proved them wrong, and that was that.

She was also absolutely filthy.

She was going to need to take a shower again, but she didn't mind. It would give her more time to soak in the wonderfulness of the moment. To turn over every detail ad nauseam until the whole thing was memorized. She—

Nova was so absorbed in her thoughts and her protesting muscles that she hadn't exactly been paying attention to where she was going. One moment she was walking, the next she collided with something very solid.

"*Ow!*"

She bounced off the thing, rubbing her nose as her eyes watered. Had someone suddenly erected a wall on her usual path? Oh, nope, it was Sal.

"Sorry," Nova said automatically before it clicked in her brain exactly who she was talking to. *Oh.*

He didn't say anything for a moment, instead staring in that very strange way of his, the same stilted look he had given her at the end of their conversation in the barn. For being such a handsome guy, he sure was awkward.

Or maybe that was just how he was around people he hated. Oh well, no skin off Nova's nose.

"Are you alright?"

"What? Oh, yeah, I'm fine. This blood isn't mine. Birthing, you know, messy business." She hadn't expected him to show concern, but it was good to know that he cared about if she was bleeding or not—even if it surprised her that he did.

"Blood? What? Oh, no. I meant your leg."

Her leg? What did he mean?

Right, what had happened in the barn. She didn't mean to, but a laugh escaped her as she shook her head. "You don't have to worry about that, friend. My knee has a mind of its own, and I've popped it back in so many times I can do it blindfolded. I'm just sore from physical therapy and then rushing down here."

But Sal didn't respond right away, still looking at her with a befuddled expression. "Why don't you just... fix it?"

It was then that it all it clicked in Nova's head. He wasn't staring at her because he thought she was bizarre or he didn't understand how to talk to someone who worked for him, it was because he was genuinely confused about the situation. She'd heard about the rich being out of touch, but she'd kind of forgotten because of not knowing any actual rich people.

"Surgery is painful and not exactly a guarantee. My knee could just keep doing the same thing. Besides, even if it was a one-hundred-percent deal, I can't exactly take all the time off work that's needed for the recovery. You really can't do *anything* while your knee is healing."

"You could save up enough money to be able to take off work for a little while, right?"

She blinked at him, but then that blinking turned into another laugh and she just shook her head. "Funny, very funny," she said with a chuckle, heading to her car. And as she walked, it didn't take long for her mind to drift away from giant ranch heir and head right back to the beautiful life she'd helped come into the world.

Her luck really was changing for the better. She could *feel* it.

7

Salvatore

Sal rubbed his face with his hands, suppressing the growl that he was building in his chest. He was *smart*! He'd always had good grades, he was witty, and never had an issue understanding new ideas. So why was he struggling so hard to put together a plan to help his dad?

Solomon and Silas both had made it seem so easy for years, but Sal found himself struggling to know which direction to go, who to contact, and how to build alliances. He felt like he was playing chess against grand masters and had only just learned how to play the game.

Even Sterling, who usually had all the ambition of a rock and couldn't even get himself together enough to sleep through the night, had flourished in his personal projects. His soil experiment was going strong, and Mom often went on and on about how he saved her tomatoes, and the vet thing was... well, it was a thing.

But Sal was struggling to even find a foundation to build his strategy on. And the fact that it was frustrating him just made him more frustrated, turning it into a never-ending cycle that built on itself in a swirling frenzy.

Ugh.

Despite what some people might think, Sal didn't *like* being angry. It made him sweat, made his heart pound and his stomach twist. If he had his way, everything would go back to normal and he could return to being the chill, somewhat vain brother who helped everyone else out when they needed some extra hands.

But that clearly wasn't going to be anytime soon, so he needed to find a way to calm down before he made himself nauseous.

Maybe some good workout endorphins would be the answer. Changing into some workout clothes, he headed outside for a jog.

Running wasn't really his thing, per se. Sure, he got his cardio in enough to be healthy, but he preferred lifting and working up some real muscle fatigue. But maybe shaking up his workout regiment would help get him out of his foul mood.

So, he hit one of the thin trails that led out into the fields. There had been a time, in high school mostly, that he and his brothers had gone on runs or hikes, and that had created strong trails that hinted at the adventures they'd gone on. But in the years since, they'd faded to barely-there paths that were rarely used by workers, only when they didn't want to take the main trail for whatever reason.

He didn't even have his headphones in, just listening to the rasp of his breath and the pound of his feet against the earth as he jogged along. He wasn't going for speed, but rather for establishing a rhythm and sticking to it, controlling his breath, controlling his pace, controlling *something* since everything seemed to be spinning so quickly out of his and his father's grip.

He hated feeling out of control. It was why he'd started packing on muscle in the first place.

It wasn't difficult to get lost to the burning of his lungs, the pounding of his feet, the smell of the fields in his nose. It had been ages since he'd been in the fields at all, and he didn't realize just how far he'd reached until he was surrounded by tall wheat, their crop farthest from the house.

Huh. Maybe he needed to run more often. It was the most peace his brain had had in what felt like weeks.

Turning around, he went to head back home when he heard the softest little lilt in the air. It wasn't anything big, but it sounded almost like a songbird that was hanging out low to the ground for some reason.

Curious, he tilted his head, listening for the next call. It came a few moments later, and he cautiously crept towards it, figuring he could use the time to catch his breath again before he headed for home.

But as he grew closer, he realized the sound was too rhythmic for any sort of bird call, and a few steps after that he realized it was singing. Soft, gentle singing that wound through the tall wheat like vines, wrapping around and caressing whatever the notes came in contact with.

It was almost haunting, in a way, and Sal couldn't help but wonder who on earth would be out at the edge of their lands singing away like some sort of beautiful ocean siren.

He wasn't sure what to think of the entire situation, but just about the last thing he expected was to part some of the wheat and make out that tall, tackle-happy worker standing next to Silas' injured horse. Her back was to him, but it was clear that she was gently petting the beast as she sang, her voice being carried on the breeze to filter out into the field.

Sal couldn't help but wonder why she was standing with a horse in the middle of a field when he vaguely remembered that his brother's horse, Amaranth, had taken a bad fall some time back. He'd heard noise about her physical therapy, but he hadn't given it much thought beyond that.

The woman started another verse, her accent coming through more thickly as she went on. It wasn't anything he'd heard before, so he guessed that it was some sort of folksy song from wherever it was she came from.

He didn't quite understand the why of it all, but he found himself transfixed by the woman as she sang, leaning her head gently against the horse's head as she ran her fingers through its mane. She was dressed in a pair of loose, cheap-looking sweats and an oversized, dark T-shirt. Nothing special to look at and certainly nothing that should have captivated him like he was.

Without thinking, his eyes slid down her body to the leg that she had injured. Her weight was definitely shifted mainly to her other foot, but she looked like she was mostly alright. Her words played through his head, where she said that she couldn't afford the time off to get better. Was that a thing? Certainly, she could get unemployment or just save up enough for things. She had to be terrible with money to not be able to have enough for recovery.

Her song ended, and for a moment there was silence. Sal was suddenly acutely aware of how large he was and that he wasn't exactly quiet when he moved. He didn't think he could step away without her noticing, and for some reason the thought of her knowing that he had been standing there, gawking at her, was far too embarrassing.

"Hey there, my beautiful girl," she cooed, her voice soft, kind. "You feeling better, yeah? You just needed to stretch your legs, right? Get out from under mom and dad who keep hovering around and babying you all the time, right my beauty?"

Amaranth let out a pointed breath, as if she were agreeing. Sal remembered when his old giant mount Bucephalus— Bruce for short—would express his opinion with noises that were so close to human emotion that it made him wonder just how much the horse understood.

"When's the last time you had someone act normal around you, huh? Well, don't worry. I'm not going to wrap you up in cotton and baby you. We can be regular friends." Amaranth waffled, because of course. "Hey, did you hear about the equestrian who went on a vacation suddenly?"

It felt like his mind was spinning, trying to figure out how to align the angry, yelling woman who tackled him with the sweet-talking lady who was laughing and patient with an injured horse. He almost wondered if she was a twin too and he had somehow met the evil one first.

"It was a *spur of the moment* decision. Get it? Get it?"

This time Amaranth didn't say anything, simply walking a few steps forward.

"Oh, I see, you're holding back your unbridled enthusiasm for my horse puns. Fair, fair. You can't let too much out of the bag at first."

Sal wasn't quite sure how long he would have stayed there if his phone didn't buzz in a way that seemed just about ten thousand times louder than it ever had been before. Swearing under his breath, he backed up and quickly hurried off.

"Hey, is someone there? That you, Alfonso?"

No, it certainly wasn't Alfonso. Sal had no interest in her finding out it was actually a Miller snooping on her, so he picked up the pace, putting distance between them but sticking to the taller crops so she wouldn't be able to see him.

...which would be a lot easier to do if he wasn't six and a half feet.

It wasn't until he was almost halfway to the house that his mind caught up with what he was doing, and he couldn't help but wonder at himself. It was *his* property. She was *his* family's employee taking care of *his* brother's horse. As far as any logic went, she was the interloper. The intruder. The one who should have been embarrassed at being caught singing and telling puns to an animal that didn't understand her.

But from the few interactions he'd had with the truly strange young woman, he had a feeling that it was only him that would leave the conversation with pink cheeks. His mind kept flicking, imagining the horribly awkward conversation that would ensue if she had caught him and the image of her standing there, golden light bathing down onto her olive skin as a beautiful melody slipped from her lips.

So much for a relaxing run.

8

Salvatore

*S*al wondered if he had enough grip strength to pull his own hair out.

A strange thing to wonder, probably, but he was stuck on yet another email and was sure that at any moment he was going to absolutely lose it. Time was running out, and he felt no closer to doing what his dad needed him to do by saving the day and getting things returned back to normal.

And what was worse was that his mind kept drifting back to that strange woman and his brother's horse. It had been a couple days and the incident should have been long gone from his memory, and yet it wasn't. At all. But every so often, he would look out the window and wonder if she was in the fields again, telling terrible jokes and talking more kind to a horse than she ever had to him.

Ugh, he was getting sidetracked again. And he could absolutely not afford that considering the latest move his brothers had pulled.

Because *of course* they had put together some solid proposals that were very appealing to some of the board of directors. Not enough to threaten a full-on coup, but enough to be... *wary*. Naturally, Dad had the final say in his empire, so it wasn't like they could force his hand in an outright sense, but there was a balance.

If there was one thing Sal had learned, was that there was always a *balance*. Yeah, Dad owned the company, founded it, said what stayed and what didn't. But if he didn't keep the board of directors happy, they could choose to leave for positions where they would be appreciated. And while some overturn was always expected, if half of them up n' went, well, that certainly wouldn't look good to the many investors for all the little pies Dad had his fingers in. And if the investors weren't happy, well, that was the first in several steps that could cause a downward spiral in profits that nobody wanted.

That was one of the most frustrating parts to Sal. He couldn't figure out why his brothers were doing what they were doing. Didn't they like being rich? Didn't they like having nice things? Why was it a bad thing to enjoy all of the fruits of their father's labor?

He didn't get it. He didn't get it at all, and it made him feel like an outsider in his own family.

Then again, he supposed he'd never *really* fit in. Too young, too gawky, then too big. He went to a college too far but returned too quickly, had been too easy-going about letting his older brothers take on so much of the responsibility. As a result, they had years of experience under their belts while he felt like he was grasping at straws.

No, it made him feel like he was outclassed, outmatched,

outsmarted, and that just made him *mad.* So mad, in fact, that he wasn't aware of what his body was doing until a sharp crack startled him out of his fuming.

Startled, Sal looked down to see that his mouse was in pieces around him, a crumpled mass of it in his large palm.

Oh.

Maybe he could use some fresh air.

Pushing himself away from his desk so fast that his chair toppled over, Sal headed outside. He felt too big for his skin, like he was going to burst from the inside out at any moment. Which, naturally, was a pretty awful sensation.

He made it out of the front door without running into anybody else, not that surprising considering his brothers were probably all out with their girls. Well, except for Sterling, who most likely wasn't up from his second sleep yet. But as he stood there, breathing in deeply through his nose and then out through his mouth, it wasn't really helping much.

And the worst part was that he knew why he was so angry. He was angry because all of his brothers were making him feel small. And he hadn't spent so much time building his muscle and training just to be reduced down to a... a... an afterthought.

Nope, the fresh air definitely wasn't helping. He needed to exert himself. Work up a sweat. But also, maybe be productive?

...did Sal know how to do anything productive?

That was a sobering thought. But a real one. Solomon was off apparently saving the city's poor with the French girl. Silas had turned himself into something of a handyman in the past year. And Sterling would go do something with Elizabeth and the animals once he woke up. All of them had physical tasks and abilities, but Sal just...

Sal was a strongman with nothing to show for it.

Since when did he have such depressing thoughts? He liked himself. He loved his life. So why did it suddenly feel so very empty?

Wood. He could cut wood. Sure, his family hardly used it anymore, but that didn't mean that he couldn't grab a few of the short logs laying around and stock things up.

The wood hutch was in the back of the house. They really only used it to store enough fuel for bonfires and fun get-togethers, considering all of their wood stoves had been removed from the manor as it grew from a regular house to a mansion.

Granted, now that those city women were around so much, his brothers had been using it more. No doubt for romantic nights looking up at the stars or warm bonfires on crisp nights. How predictable.

...actually, when Sal thought about it, that didn't sound *so* bad.

Shaking his head, he pulled his shirt off and threw it to the side, unlocking the ax from its steel case against the house by punching in the combination and grabbing his first log. He was rusty, but after a few tries, he fell back into the same rhythms from high school, not too differently from how he had sunken into jogging.

A swing, a crack, his muscles burning as he went through the motions. Breathe in. Breathe out. Inhale, exhale. It was all a cycle, and one he was good at. Maybe he couldn't figure out how to stop his brothers' mad campaign, but he could chop wood.

It was soothing and he felt his anger abate. He wished he had brought his headphones out so that he could listen to something while he was working through whatever was going on with himself, but he'd left them curled in a fairly dense knot right beside his bed. He had spares, of course, but most of them were sitting in a pile in his personal gym, where he tended to leave them after a good workout.

Oh well, it was nice to listen to the rush of his breath, the sharp, crisp crack of wood splitting. The birds chirping around him and the wind gently blowing. It was peaceful. Kind of reminded him of a time when he was young, when there was so much possibility in the world and his family actually felt like a family.

He was immersed in the ritual of it all, certain he was alone, until a sharp gasp startled him. Raising his ax like some sort of threat, he jerked and looked around for the source of the very human sound.

Sure enough, there was the strange, tackle-happy woman standing there with a bucket, one of her hands covering her eyes. Her shoulders were nearly up to her ears, and he could see her cheeks coloring pink behind her palm.

Huh, for once she actually looked flustered. How about that.

"What are you doing?" Sal asked gruffly. Of course, it was just his luck that the one person he *really* wanted to avoid had ended up in the place where he was trying to get away from his swirling thoughts.

"I was just out collecting some of the lizards!" Her voice was more shrill than he'd ever heard it before. Huh, it looked like the woman was actually able to be ruffled; it just took some skin.

"The lizards?" he asked, leaning forward to see if he could make out what was in her bucket.

"Uh, yeah. I wanted to grab a few and put them in a part of the ranch where Elizabeth and I are trying to restore more of the natural ecology."

He took a step forward, noting her hand did *not* move from her eyes. Which was silly. He was shirtless, yeah, but he was a man. It wasn't anything different from what one would see at the beach. But his curiosity at her reaction was waylaid when he realized that it was indeed little lizards in her tall pail.

"You're not creeped out by them?"

Sal was neither here nor there with lizards. They just kinda existed. But he had plenty of memories of girls in school screaming when one skittered out of the equipment bin, or when several would join in at bonfires to absorb some of the warmth.

"What? Creeped out? No, I love reptiles. Geckos are probably my favorite, but these lil' guys are cute too." She took her hand away from her eyes, a broad smile on her face, only to yelp when she realized he was closer than ever and still shirtless. "Oi, put on a shirt, will you?"

That... that wasn't what Sal was used to.

Ever since he had packed on the muscle and shot up, he was used to people appreciating his physique. And when he took his shirt off for swimming, certainly no one complained. But the woman didn't sound intrigued or pleased at all.

But she did sound nervous.

Was she *shy*?

That seemed about just the most impossible thing, but her cheeks were *really* red. Seizing the opportunity to see if he could finally fluster the strange woman, he took another step closer. Maybe she wasn't as different from other women as she liked to pretend.

"I don't hear you putting a shirt on," she said, the corners of her full lips tucking down into a frown.

"Because I'm not." Another step forward. Not enough to be threatening, that was just about the opposite of what he wanted, but it was enough to put them at a conversational distance. "It's pretty hot out and I've worked up quite a sweat, so it seems counterintuitive to do so."

"Counterintuitive, huh?"

"Yeah, wouldn't you say so?"

"I'd say it was inappropriate, mate. You're my boss, and I shouldn't be seeing your pecs. That's just... that's *weird*. Like, too casual."

Hah, she really *was* flustered. It almost would have been adorable if it came from anyone else.

"What's wrong with being casual from time to time? I didn't know chopping wood was a formal affair."

He was so sure that he was gaining ground, that her cheeks would go scarlet and she'd reach that level of super-flustered where she would stutter and maybe even sweat. But instead she just sighed, her hand dropping away from her eyes.

When her gaze landed squarely on his face and nowhere else, there was irritation there. "Do you think I'm totally clueless?" she asked, tone biting.

Sal stared a solid beat longer than he should of. "Do I— what?"

"Whatever," was all she replied before storming off, leaving Sal blinking at where she and her lizard bucket had been.

...was it a European thing, or had the strangest woman in the world just so happened to invade his family's ranch?

9

Nova

*A*nother month on the ranch.

It was wonderful. She was learning *so* much. The kind of stuff that she would pay thousands of dollars to learn in veterinary school. She wasn't sure if Elizabeth knew it or not, but she really was providing a valuable education that was going to get Nova ahead.

Actually, even *more* ahead, because having a steady, full-time paycheck was doing her wonders. She had caught up on all of her bills and was saving up for a new car. Well, new to *her*. She wasn't about to pop over to a dealership, but she was pretty sure she could buy a used one off someone. And then she'd be sitting pretty.

Sure, she still pretty much came home every day completely sore and wiped out, but it was a good kind of exhaustion. The kind that came from accomplishing things and feeling productive. Her knee hadn't dislocated in a good while, although she still definitely got shooting pains down her calf and up her thigh at different times. At least they usually never happened at the same time. Those days were the *worst.*

Everything was going great. Really, the only thing she would change was just how much she ran into that Sal character.

It had been two weeks since the shirt incident, and she couldn't get it out of her mind—which was incredibly embarrassing. But the man was *ripped.* Like... impossibly so. He was like something out of an action or superhero movie, all perfectly carved muscles and shining skin. He was a completely unfair combination of devastatingly handsome and powerful.

She'd been gobsmacked at first, because how could she not be? He was such a *hunk!* But then she'd realized that he was using his looks just to get a rise out of her and wow, had that ticked her off more than anything else.

She hated being manipulated.

When Nova had been younger, she'd been lanky, gawkish, and hadn't quite grown into her features. Always the ugly duckling, kids in her school had played cruel jokes by asking her out for their friend and then their friend acting grossed out. It was annoying, it was childish, and yet it always made her angry.

It wasn't until she was nineteen, just three scant years ago, that she started to grow into her looks. Her face fit her better, and she had cheekbones that sat high and regal under her dark, heavily lashed eyes. Sure, she was still pretty much flat as a board on top, with broad shoulders and defined arms, if she did say so herself. Although not Elizabeth-levels of defined.

That vet was something *else.* But Nova's thighs had thickened while her hips had widened, leaving her with a curvy lower half that some people needed a plastic surgeon's help to achieve.

So, when Sal was sidling up to her, looking all Adonis-like and glistening in the sun, there had been a sharp moment where she'd gone from addled by his straight-up impressiveness to feeling tricked. Teased. Made fun of.

She probably shouldn't have asked him if he thought she was an idiot, but it was so hard to contain her temper when she felt embarrassed. She'd stormed off, and while he hadn't approached her since, they still crossed paths annoyingly often. If she had her way, she'd just forget he even existed.

...which was difficult considering how his chiseled torso kept popping into her mind's eye. *Inconvenient.*

At least the horses didn't judge her for mentally ogling the guy. They only cared if she brought them treats, which of course she did. She wasn't cruel, after all.

"I'm weak, Obelisk," Nova groaned, letting her head rest against Sterling's horse's flank. The poor Miller boy was down with what appeared to be the flu, so she had been more than happy to spend some extra time riding the mount at the start of her shift then spending a good chunk of time brushing out his coat when they were done. Obelisk was a good horse, even if he had a saucy attitude, and he definitely liked to try to lead if she didn't pay close attention. "I think the Bible says I'm supposed to pluck out my own eyes or something, right? If I can't keep them to myself? Pretty sure Jesus said that."

"What's this about plucking out eyeballs? I'm pretty sure our insurance won't cover that if it's self-inflicted."

Nova yelped, nearly dropping the curry comb that she had been using. She had forgotten that Silas was in the barn with her, baby-talking to his horse. He'd been quiet after telling her he was getting a bottle of water from the mini fridge on the far side of the building.

Well, that was absolutely embarrassing.

"Oh, nothing. Just being silly with Obelisk here."

"That makes sense; he's a silly kind of boy."

"Is he? I hadn't noticed." Whew, there was one bullet dodged. As nice as Silas seemed, it definitely didn't feel appropriate to admit that her mind kept calling up images of his younger brother's glistening abs.

...definitely not appropriate.

"He's got character, alright. Matches Sterling just fine."

"How is he doin', by the by?" Nova asked, glad they were just glossing right over the whole eye-plucking thing.

"Not bad. I mean, he's miserable, feverish and pretty much permanently wrapped up in a blanket, but Mom's feeding him soup on the regular."

"Oh, not Elizabeth?"

"She tried, actually, but Sterling didn't want her getting sick and told her she was temporarily banned from the house."

Nova laughed at that. Elizabeth always seemed so determined and in charge that it was hard to imagine her listening to an order from a sick man.

"And she actually listened to him?"

"Yup. Funny thing about those two. They're both stubborn as brick walls, but somehow, they know when they need to bend for each other. Never thought anyone would get my twin besides me, but Miss Elizabeth certainly has a way with him."

"You like her?" Nova said, looking over the horse. "Not like, romantically, but in that annoying older brother who approves kinda way?"

The smile he gave her over Amaranth's back was a genuine one. No wonder he'd been able to bag that smoking hot mechanic that had looked at Nova's junker. "Yeah. I think they're bringing out the best in each other. Then again, I might be biased."

"Why, because he's your twin?"

"Nah, because it was after they started dating that my brother really started talking to me again."

"...oh?" There was a story there, that was for sure. As far as Nova knew, the twins got on like white on rice, all finishing each other's sentences and being buddy-buddy, but the way Silas had worded that made it seem like that hadn't always been the case.

"Ah, it's all in the past. Nothing we need to worry about now. But yes, I like Elizabeth in that annoying older brother kind of way."

"What about being an annoying older brother?"

Nova cringed and ducked right back behind Obelisk's neck, gently resting her forehead against his soft fur. She knew that voice without having to even see that irritatingly handsome face on that oh-so-good-looking body of his.

"Hey Sal, you need something? Or did you swing around just to take in the sights..."

Nova peeked around the horse, sensing the tension ramping up in the air, and it wasn't because of her. There was *definitely* something going on with the brothers that she wasn't entirely privy to.

"Do I need a reason to come see the horses?"

Yeah, tension. *So* much tension.

"No, just not a place I see you too often."

"Yeah, I guess we don't see each other that often much."

"I guess we don't."

Nova peeked out further just to accidentally make eye contact with Sal, like he had been looking at her the entire time instead of the brother he was barbing back and forth with. Ducking her head, she returned to her grooming of Obelisk.

At least the horse was tolerating the lengthy grooming like a champ. He had every right to be overstimulated, but he seemed to be a fairly chill mount. Either that or he was enjoying the soap-opera-like drama going on.

But Nova certainly wasn't. She could feel his gaze on her, not fading, even as he and Silas kept right on doing whatever it was they were doing. She was so busy pretending to be busy and completely oblivious to things that she didn't realize Sal had approached her until he cleared his throat right by the opening of the stall.

"Oh!" she blurted with a start, dropping the curry comb for real this time and scrambling to catch it. She bounced it between her hands for a moment before it clattered to the ground. Nova picked it up, huffing when she saw that Sal was still there, looking amused.

"You okay there?"

"Just peachy. You need something?"

"Why does everyone keep asking me that?"

"Maybe because you're being right weird," she said before she could think better of it. Geez, her mum was right; her mouth was going to get her in trouble.

"Funny, coming from the woman who freaked out because of a little PG-rated nudity."

Ugh. How annoying. "Sure, freaking out. That's what I did."

"Didn't you?"

"I remember it differently."

"And how is that?"

"I remember that you were being rude and highly unprofessional, and I had to leave the situation."

He frowned. Good. Too bad that didn't make him look any less handsome. "Come on, it wasn't like that."

"Wasn't it?" she shot right back.

"I—"

"Look, if you're here to apologize, then do it. Otherwise, I have work to do."

"Apologize? For being shirtless on my own property?"

She leveled him with a *look*. Sure, maybe she was being overly particular, but she was never the type of girl to fraternize with her employer. And while she didn't mind him taking off his shirt for some heavy work, she didn't like how he'd acted once he'd noticed that she was... kerfuffled.

When she didn't answer beyond that, he huffed, actually *huffed*. "Whatever," was all he said, echoing the ending of their last interaction, before turning on his heel and heading back out of the barn.

"Hey, you alright over there?"

Nova took a deep breath and looked to Silas, who had a keen sort of expression on his face. Oh right, he had seen all of that. How mortifying.

"I'm fine," she said quickly. "I know how to handle a guy like him."

"A guy like him?"

Uh-oh. Right, even if Silas seemed like a nice person, she needed to remember that he was Sal's brother. He would be way more loyal to him than her. "Oh, you know. The macho, confident type who's never experienced the real world."

"Ah, yes. Then that would be Sal, alright."

Whew, crisis averted. Maybe she shouldn't have been paranoid considering the tension between the two, but one never knew with family. It could have been one of those cases where Silas was allowed to trash talk his brother, but an employee certainly wasn't.

Much to her relief, Silas dropped it and went back to babying Amaranth. She finished up with Obelisk and moved on to the other horses. Apparently, Elizabeth had put several through their paces out in the ring, so they could use a dose of encouragement and maybe some extra brushing. Nova slid into the care, going through the mental checklist the vet had taught her. The minutes slipped by and, before she knew it, Silas was knocking at the side of the stall that she was in.

"Hey, it started raining so I closed the barn doors. Do you want a ride to your car?"

Nova blinked, looking up at the ceiling as if that would tell her what the weather was outside. A beat later, she realized she could hear the gentle pitter-patter of a soft rain.

"Nah, I still have a few more hours of work left."

"You sure?"

"Yeah, I'll be fine." She sent him what she hoped was an amiable grin. "Besides, a little rain never killed anyone."

"Tell that to Noah."

"Um, I'm pretty sure that was a *lot* of rain."

"Right. Thankfully this doesn't seem to be ark levels. I'll see you around, Nova."

"See you around, boss."

"Just call me Silas, please."

Nova nodded. In all honesty, Silas came across as too casual for one of her bosses. Especially considering that he was the one that she saw the most.

The Miller son walked out, the sound of rain increasing as he opened the door to exit before being muffled again. Nova loved when it stormed and the smell of the earth after. It reminded her of home, of gray days spent curled up with a book in the attic, pressed up against the window as she tried to carve away her own little escape from her family.

A frown forced its way onto her features, as it often did whenever she thought of home. There were so many things she missed, fish and chips, good tea, the sense of community, but there were also so many things she didn't. At all. Like everything about her past, there was a complex mix of positive and negative that couldn't be separated from each other. She could remember the time her family had all traveled to the beach, laughing and splashing. But she could also remember her mother's comment about Nova needing to stop wearing shorts because she was getting fat.

Fat. She was fifteen at the time and barely a size two. But she'd been a size double zero for so long, the change as she went through puberty was definitely noticeable. And while Nova had eventually learned that there was nothing wrong with being a little heavier built, when she'd been a teen that offhanded comment had been devastating.

There was the time where she had really worked extra hard to make the honor's list in her junior year of high school, a difficult thing to do considering all the advanced classes she was taking for college credit. But when she presented her certificate to her parents, they just asked why she hadn't always been getting such good grades since she was clearly capable.

...ugh.

She wished she could wash away all the bad, but it didn't work like that. Maybe that was one of the reasons the pros and cons of rain felt so familiar. Sure, it was gray and cold, and everything got soaked, but also it was life-giving, cleansing, and soothing. Couldn't have the good without the bad. The bad without the good.

Her pondering and helping the horses had time slipping by far faster than it had any right to, and the next thing she knew, her phone alarm was going off in the pocket of her overalls, signaling that it was time to stop for the day. Wow. Nova had never had a job where her eyes weren't constantly glued to the clock, praying to make it to the end of her shift. But working for the Millers was amazing. Even if they had some weird, rich-people drama going on.

Finishing up, she headed outside. Making sure her phone was tucked deep into her pocket, she tilted her face up to catch some of the rain.

It was slightly warm, although it would cool quickly as it streaked down her face. But it was nice nonetheless, twisty memories and all.

Before she could get soaked, she headed back to her car, enjoying the stroll. Since working at the Millers, she'd found that she'd been able to slow down much more often. Sure, she still worked as hard as she could while on the clock, but she found herself arriving early so she could mosey to wherever she needed to be, and then taking her time leaving. It was so different than any job she'd had before, but she absolutely loved it. She couldn't have been more grateful.

A sighing sort of laugh bubbled up from her mouth. When was the last time that she had been so happy? She couldn't say. Lifting her arms, she spun around, tilting her wet face back up again.

"Thank you!" she called to the sky. Or maybe God. She wasn't sure. All she knew was that there was a warmth in her that—

THUMP!

Nova's vision spun and all the breath was driven from her body. Breathing jaggedly, it took her a moment to figure out that she was suddenly on her back in the mud.

... how had that happened?

One moment she had been walking and then she was prone on the ground. It wasn't until a beat later that her knee began to throb, and she put two and two together.

Drat. And she'd been doing so *good*.

Groaning, Nova pushed herself up. Her butt and back were soaked, but that hardly registered over the intense pain radiating from her leg. A few curses bubbled up before she finally managed to get herself into a sitting position, looking down at her now-muddy knee.

"You did that on purpose," she accused, narrowing her gaze.

The knee did not answer back, although she supposed it would have been much more alarming if it had. Gripping it on either side, she jerked it quickly back into place the same as usual.

... or at least she *tried* to, but with the wet and the mud, her hands slipped, leaving her yelping out in surprise and pain with a still-busted knee.

Ow.

"Come on. Work with me."

She gripped it again, but it was angry with her for messing it up once. Securing the placement of her hands, she tried the same twist and shove.

OW!

Nope, that hadn't worked. That hadn't worked at all.

The comparative cool that Nova was usually able to keep whenever her body did something annoying quickly began to evaporate. She could try getting up, but she knew from experience that it was both excruciating and very difficult to do with a bum knee. Especially since she was in a grassy area between barns. There wasn't really anything for her to grip or grab to help her up.

She was stuck. Just great. She was going to need help. She hoped Elizabeth wouldn't hold it against her. After all, Nova had promised that she could handle herself.

Reaching into her pocket for her janky phone, she pulled it out to see not only was it cracked, but it was soaked, and mud had seeped through her pants while she was trying to get her knee into place.

...well, that was certainly not a good development.

There was that panic again, burning bright and making her nauseous. Nova swallowed it down, telling herself that she could do all of that later. At the moment, she needed to concentrate on problem-solving.

But she didn't even have that much time to order her thoughts because a shadow loomed over her, which was particularly impressive considering just how gray it was. Tilting her head back, she saw, of course, it was none other than Sal.

What was with her luck?

"Here," he said, offering one of his truly massive hands. "Let me help you up."

"I'm fine," she answered tersely. She was *not* about to play the damsel in distress. Gripping her knee again, she hastily jerked it, only for her hand to slip and her nail to score a smarting line down the side of her other palm.

"*Blimey!*" she snapped, her temper flaring. She had truly jinxed herself by being too happy for too many consecutive minutes. Exasperated, she heaved her weight to the side to see if she could sort of roll onto her front then push herself up onto one leg. What she would do once she was on one leg, she didn't know, but it would at least be progress.

Except she never quite got to one leg, because the next thing she knew, she was being picked up and thrown over one truly muscled shoulder.

"What are you doing?" Nova asked, hissing as her knee bounced against his torso. A human's front shouldn't be as hard as a rock!

At hearing her sound of pain, the giant of a man changed his grip, supporting her thigh and calf so that her leg didn't jiggle. "I would have thought that much was obvious."

"You're hilarious. Put me down!"

"I will. Just not in the middle of a muddy path where you'll be stranded. Now stop wiggling; I don't want you messing up your leg even more."

Her cheeks burned, her stomach twisted, and she was all too acutely aware of the musculature pressed up against her body. Her protests faded, though, and eventually they passed through a doorway.

Out of the rain, she took a moment to shake her head, water flicking everywhere from her choppy pixie cut. Of course, that movement had her looking down, and she couldn't help but notice that Sal's backside was just as impressive as his front side.

Huh, God really was unfair sometimes.

He let out a small grunt, interrupting her accidental ogling, and then she was being set down on something relatively high up. Enough for her feet to dangle off the floor, which was something considering that she was at least sixty percent legs. Looking around, she realized they were in the mechanic's garage, a place she'd only gone to once before when Teddy needed to borrow her for a quick errand.

Licking her lips, her gaze finally returned to her unexpected hero. Her position on the tool table had them seeing eye to eye, something she wasn't quite used to. He was giving her quite the intense stare, one that made her equally want to stick out her tongue at him or run away and hide.

"Uh, thanks?" she said, feeling uncertain. She was covered in mud and soaked and surely looked a right mess while he could have subbed in for some sort of movie star in a romantic scene where he'd just been caught in the perfect drizzle.

"What do you need to fix yourself?"

"What? Oh... a towel would be a good start. And an ice pack. I think bringing down the swelling will help me get it back in place." Also, it would take an edge of the pain off. Because with each passing minute, Nova was more and more aware of just how much her leg was throbbing.

"Okay." He gave her a solid nod then turned to walk off, no doubt to get her the things that she had asked for. Sure, she was irritated at being manhandled and thrown over his shoulder like a sack of potatoes, but she was pleased that he was listening to her directions without second-guessing her. He didn't try to tell her what to do or lecture her on being careless. He asked what she needed, and it seemed like he was going to get it.

But still, what a strange dude.

10

Salvatore

Crack!

Sal watched as the woman popped her knee back into place, wincing at the rather dramatic noise. She, however, didn't seem to think anything of it, pressing one of the ice packs he'd gotten her against her knee while grumbling something about the joint being extra angry.

"Is that why you have a limp?" he heard himself ask before thinking better of it. On second thought, probably not the best way to start the conversation. But he found himself at a loss. He'd gone to the horses hoping to find her, to see if he could decipher what had turned her mood so sour at their last meeting, only for her to basically accuse him of being a real jerk and dismissing him. If he hadn't been so irritated with her actions, he wouldn't have left his nice, filtered water bottle behind. And if he hadn't left that behind, then he wouldn't have gone back to the barn to get it and stumbled across the injured woman literally stuck in the mud.

Needless to say, it'd been a very interesting day.

And that wasn't even taking into account everything that had happened after that. She'd brushed him off at first—somewhat predictably—and tried to do that horrible knee-twisting thing she did before. It didn't work, something he guessed had to do with the mud and rain, but she kept on trying, but each time she let out truly awful sounds of pain and misery.

It had been too much for him. Before he could even think it through, he was picking her up and hauling her towards what had once been Teddy's mechanic garage, but which had become more of a general garage since she had stopped being a contracted employee.

Nova was solid—that much he'd figured from when she'd barreled into him. But he had pointedly ignored how his broad palm felt against the back of her strong thighs as he held her to him, his other hand busy holding her calve to stop her injured knee from jostling. His whole focus had been only on getting her to safety as quickly as possible and getting her to safety with as little jiggling as possible. Two goals that certainly seemed contradictory.

"No, I've had that limp since I was a teen."

"Oh."

He hadn't expected her to continue, especially considering the tempestuous nature of all of their other interactions, but she did anyway. "I was in a car accident when I was younger. My knee started hurting real bad, but my parents didn't believe me when I told them how much pain I was in and refused to take me to a doctor. Work apparently was super busy." She huffed out a sound and if that wasn't just about the most bitter thing Sal had ever heard. "And wouldn't you know, walking around on a shattered kneecap for over a year can cause lasting damage. Absolutely wild."

"You walked around on a shattered kneecap for an entire year?"

"Well... walking is a generous term. I used crutches for six months until people accused me of using them too long—and they started to give me wicked tension headaches in my shoulders as it is—so then I hobbled, limped, and wobbled around until finally I got to see someone."

"I thought the UK was supposed to have miraculous universal healthcare that can fix anything."

The look she gave him was sharp, almost as cold as the ice pack she was holding. "Mate, I lived at a military base at the time and all my doctors were from the States. I *wish* I had some of that sweet NHS healthcare that my buddies did. Goodness knows their mums didn't have to wrestle with Tricare every other emergency."

Sal felt his eyebrows shoot up. "You were an army brat?"

"Heavy on the brat, light on that whole military part. Ended up really being not my bag."

"So... were you born in the States?"

"Nope. On a base. I've lived everywhere, mind you. Guam, Japan, but the largest chunk of my life was Britain, and now that my dad's retired from military life, that's where they've chosen to settle. That's why I've got the accent too. Though the thing's certainly faded from living here for a while. Think I'll ever get a southern drawl?"

"I, uh..." He tried to think of her speaking with any sort of thick, American-esque accent and it just sounded *wrong*. "Nah, I don't think so."

"Pity. Seems fun."

"Fun?"

"Yeah. Laid-back, easy-going. Sure, there's the stereotypes of being not-so-bright or racist, but those are mostly just stereotypes. I wish I was better at mimicking people because I think it'd be rather fun to sound completely different at the drop of a hat."

"...right."

It was possibly the most she had said to him that wasn't yelling at him about some sort of reptile. He found himself following the lilt of her voice, the gentle up and down of it, the way she emphasized different words than he would have. It made him wonder why she would ever want to sound like anything else.

"Hey, I thought I saw a mini fridge in here once. Is there a fresh water bottle in it? My mouth always gets super dry after one of these spells."

"It's the adrenaline," Sal heard himself answer automatically as his feet took him around to where the fridge was.

"Oh, is it? That makes sense. I get that way during tests sometimes. I don't miss that about high school."

"You tellin' me you weren't a scholastic shining star?"

Was he bantering? It certainly felt like banter. Except it was with the bizarre, reptile-loving employee who seemed to be irritated by everything he did, so that couldn't be right.

"Excuse you. I earned respectable grades most of the time. And apparently, compared to American education, I did *right* well."

"As opposed to the left well?"

"Oh man, do you really want to get into teasing about

colloquialisms when I've literally heard people around here unironically use a triple contraction."

"A triple what?" Sal said, tossing her the water bottle and quickly draining one of his own.

"Contraction. Don't tell me you've never heard someone use the abomination y'all'd've, because I know you're a liar."

Sal laughed, which surprised him more than it should have. "That's more of a deep south thing in Alabama and the likes, but yeah, I suppose I've heard it a few times."

"I rest my case."

"Which was?"

"That people in glass houses would do well not to throw stones." Unlike every other time they'd spoken, the woman had an easy smile on her face. It made her features light up, showing off her high cheekbones and pouty lips. Sal knew that blond with bright eyes was what was in at the moment, but there was something about her dark hair and deep, chocolate eyes that drew him in.

Not that he was drawn in! No, not at all. She was an *employee*. But still, he wasn't *blind*. He could see that she was a fairly attractive lady when she wasn't tackling folks or covering half of her face with her hands.

"Hey, I don't think I ever caught your name," he said, tossing his empty bottle into the recycling. She mimicked him but winced when she missed.

"Sorry, could you get that for me? And I'm surprised to hear that. Figured you would have learned that when you tried to get me fired."

He stiffened mid-bend while retrieving her errant missile. "One of my brothers tell you that?" It figured.

She just chuckled. "Nah, mate. You did. Practically

declared it in writing when you tried to have Elizabeth fire me then stalked off to find one of the twins."

"Right." He had forgotten about that. He'd had a lot on his mind. "Look, I—"

But she held up her hands, laughing again. "You don't need to explain it. On my first day of work I tackled one of my bosses. I get it, not a good foot to start on."

...oh. That wasn't what he expected her take to be.

She continued, "Anyway, it's Nova. Nova Clark. You don't need to introduce yourself." Her smile was curled at that last comment, giving her an entirely impish look. "You can say that your reputation precedes you."

"Fair enough. You know, we don't have to be enemies, Nova."

At that, the woman's dark eyes went wide. "Enemies? Who said we were enemies?"

"Well, given how you usually act when we talk—"

"Look, I'm short with you because you're annoying and awkward, not because we're *enemies*."

"Wait, I'm awkward?" There was a lot to unpack in that statement. A bloom of happiness that she didn't consider him to be her opponent. He felt like all of his brothers considered him that, and it was so exhausting. No, that wasn't the right word. Alienating? Yeah, maybe that was it. But that happiness was quickly dimmed by her assessment that he was obnoxious.

Sal wasn't used to being called *annoying* by women. No, usually the adjectives they used for him were much more complimentary.

"Look, thanks for the help. I really do appreciate it. Now I'm gonna limp to my car, head home and maybe take a good, long soak in my terrible tub." She wrinkled her freckled nose. "Ugh, I can't fit my upper body and my lower half in at the same time, though, too tall. So I've gotta stick my legs up in the air and rest my heels against the tile or just sit when my entire upper half out of the warm water. Lame. Maybe I'll just haul my old shower-stool out of my lil' storage thing in the basement and sit awhile."

"You can't fit into the tub?" Sal didn't know why he'd been reduced to repeating her phrases or using such short sentences, but she didn't seem to notice.

"Nah, too tall and the thing is shallow as it is. Anyway, guess I better get going."

On instinct, Sal took a step forward and offered his arm. But apparently Nova hadn't expected that, because she *jumped* down from her perch, landing right in front of him.

"Whoa there!" she yelped, swaying.

Those instincts kept right on going and the arm he had meant to offer her for balance wrapped around her waist to steady her again, feeling the muscles of her back correct themselves as she regained her balance on one foot.

He could feel the blush rising up his face, making his cheeks hot as he was suddenly acutely aware of her form barely an inch away from him, the heat of her, the rise and fall of her chest with her breathing. She really *was* beautiful, in a sort of strong, rooted way.

And he could *smell* her too. There was the mixture of rain and mud, of course, but something sweeter and softer floating above it. Was it jasmine? Roses? He couldn't tell, but it hooked his attention, making him want to bury his nose in her hair and figure out exactly what it was.

He didn't do that, of course. He was sure she wouldn't react well to *that*. But he did freeze, his mind spinning as it collected thousands of little details.

"Uh… thanks, but I'm good," Nova said coolly, taking a limping step to the side and around him.

He dropped his arm immediately, embarrassed by his reaction, but the woman didn't even seem to notice. She gave him a sort of half-salute and headed back out into the rain, limping along like it was completely normal. As he watched her go, he couldn't help but wonder what the heck was going on with him.

11

Nova

Nova was baking.

Nova *never* baked, as it was something that her mum had forced onto her because "a lady should know how to bake." She was beside herself that she was making a batch of chocolate chip cookies and cupcakes.

And the whole reason she was flexing her culinary skill was because she was going to give the whole lot of sweets to Sal.

Sure, maybe she didn't really like him that much, and maybe approaching him on her own made her nervous, but he helped her fix her knee and also got her someplace safe so she could dry off enough to take care of herself. Baking him something seemed like the right thing to do.

Because while Nova knew she was stubborn and maybe

too quick to judge, one thing that no one could ever call her was *ungrateful.*

Nope, that was not on her character card, and it never was going to be, so Mr. Salvatore Miller was going to get his thank-you sweets and he was going to *like* them.

Nova nodded to herself and finished up the last of the steps with the frosting. By the time she was done with that—and had surfed on her phone a little—it was time to take the cookies out and set them aside to cool. Once that was done to her satisfaction, she shut everything down and headed out to PT, steps still uneven from how swollen and unhappy her knee was.

It was a beautiful day as she hobbled in, and she realized something while approaching the desk. For the first time in ages, she didn't have to worry about her bank account overdrafting. Thanks to her new job, she was basically rolling in money. Or at least, rolling in it compared to how she'd had to penny-pinch for years. It was a nice feeling, that was for certain. And hopefully that nice feeling was going to carry her through her PT session—because she had a feeling she was going to really be put through her paces because of the most recent incident.

She was absolutely right.

Her physical therapist was *not* happy to hear what had happened, and after looking at her knee, he had heat packs on it for twenty minutes before doing some electric stimulation. After that, it was *so* many stretches and tests to find out if there was a new muscle group acting up and causing the multiple dislocations.

It was a lot, a whole lot. Once more, Nova found herself breathing hard and flopping back on one of the mats as she worked through an exercise that involved her sticking her injured leg up in the air and trying to rotate her ankle and flexing her foot in strange ways. She felt like she shouldn't be so exhausted from what basically equated to a junior's version of a yoga class, but she was definitely feeling that.

"Oh, hello there again. Could you use some water?"

Nova removed her arm from over her eyes to see that the same older woman she'd met at a previous session was standing a bit away from her, with a cool water bottle at the ready. If there was one thing that Nova really liked about Texas, it was that people were quick to offer up some cool hydration as a sign of hospitality.

"Oh, yes, thank you."

"It's getting hotter every day, it feels like," the woman continued, handing off the drink and sitting carefully down on the mat herself. Nova wasn't quite sure what to think as she watched the relatively limber woman go through stretches as well. The young woman was used to seeing the elderly be much more... well, *frail*.

"Something like that. Thank you for the water. I thought I was going to have to drag myself to the fountain for a refill."

"We couldn't have that, now could we?" she said, a broad smile deepening the wrinkles around her eyes and making her just about the most welcoming sight Nova had seen in a while.

"Apparently not," Nova answered, feeling herself smile in return. Water bottle drained, she flopped back down, her breathing settling as she figured out how she felt about the whole Sal thing.

And by the whole Sal thing, she mostly meant how her mind kept flicking back to how strong he'd felt, lifting her like it was nothing, and that annoying image of his muscles glistening in the sun. Really, what was she, some sort of teenager?

"You look like something is on your mind."

"Do I?"

"Sure. But also, I have a knack for that sort of thing."

"You have a knack for telling when people are thinking?"

"I have a knack for telling when people are troubled."

"Ah." Nova sat up, looking over the woman again. She seemed to be a normal elderly lady. "It's silly."

"Tell me anyway."

"Well... it's kind of complicated."

"Complicated and silly? Sounds quite confusing." Her tone was just on the edge of teasing and it made Nova smile, the bundle of anxiety in her chest unraveling.

"Okay, so I know this guy."

"A guy, huh? So is this a matter of heart instead of your head?"

Nova scoffed, her nose wrinkling. "No, nothing like that. It's just uh, one of my kind-of employers is pretty... weird."

"Kind-of employer?"

"Well, his brother hired me to work on their family ranch, but I'm paid under their whole corporation so I'm just not entirely sure who is my boss and who isn't, so I just treat them all equally."

"Ah, smart. You're not the only one with a Miller brother on your mind, if that helps you feel better."

Nova's spine jolted. "What? I never said anything about the Millers!"

The woman just leveled her with a *look* while she stretched out her calf, pulling the toes of her orthotic shoes back. "Bless your heart. You don't need to say their name when you're talking about a group of rich brothers that don't see eye to eye but own a successful ranch."

"Huh," Nova grumbled. "And here I thought Dallas was supposed to be a city too big for gossip."

"Oh, there's no such thing as too big for gossip when a billionaire family is involved."

"Yeah... I guess not."

"Anyway, which brother is it that's bothering you?"

"The second youngest. Sal. I thought he was a real cad when I met him, and I'm still not entirely sure that he's not, but recently he helped me out of a bind and I felt like I got a peek that there might be a better side to him."

"Well, that's because there is."

Nova blinked, surprised at the matter-of-fact way the woman said it. Like stating that the grass was green and the days were hot. "Do you know him?"

"No, but I don't have to."

"I don't follow."

The woman's smile was sweet as she answered, exactly what someone would expect out of a loving old grandmum. Nova had never had one of those.

"I know it because everyone has the potential to be better or worse. You'll never meet anyone who is as awful or as good as they can be. So, while you absolutely saw a glimpse of something good in the young man, there's no guarantee that's the direction he'll go. But it was definitely there if you were able to notice it."

"I never thought of it that way. It sure would be great if he was able to turn it around. That little snippet of him was pretty nice, if I do admit it." She left out how it made her heart thump to think of how he'd carried her, and the intense way he'd looked her over once she was set on the mechanic's bench in front of him. She didn't think anyone had ever looked at her like *that*.

"Everyone starts their journeys at different places, you know. Sometimes what's obviously the right way to go for one person is unimaginable to another. And other times, it takes a bright light to lead people away from the darkness."

"Are you saying I should be a bright light for the lad?"

"I didn't, but it's interesting that that's the conclusion you jumped to."

For being so sweet and candid, the woman sure did have a smooth way of talking. "You some sort of retired therapist or something?"

She laughed, revealing a row of pearly white teeth. "Goodness! What a compliment. No, I'm just a gardener and a volunteer greeter at my church. Guess I've always just been blessed with ears to listen."

"That's one way to put it." Nova couldn't really remember the last time she had discussed such vulnerable things with someone. Most of her online friends and people she left back home didn't even know the name of the family she worked for. "But is it even my responsibility to assign myself as a guide to someone who has all of the resources and time in the world? Shouldn't he be more responsible for his growth himself?"

"It's not your responsibility at all. In fact, it's not anyone's beyond the young man himself. But if your mind is stuck on him, perhaps that is what you are being led to do in your heart. I don't think there's any harm in indulging that little voice, just a bit, and seeing where it leads."

"It sounds so simple when you say it," Nova murmured, shaking her head at all the thoughts rushing her.

"I've had a lot of time to see a lot of things. It certainly helps with perspective."

"Yeah, I imagine. Thank you... uh..."

"You can call me Auntie Kini, that's what most of my lil' ones call me anyway."

"Alright then, thank you, Auntie Kini." Nova didn't say it

the exact same way, her accent different from the older woman's warm lilt, but it was still pretty nice to say.

"Don't worry about it. I'm here once a week while I keep recovering from my hip replacement, so we'll have plenty of time to talk."

"I'd like that."

The woman nodded, and they fell into companionable silence. They worked until Nova's physical therapist came back to collect her for the next round of exercises. But as they parted, Nova couldn't help but turn Auntie Kini's words over and over again in her head.

12

Salvatore

*A*s you can see, it's clearly the best way to return—
No. That wasn't right.

The numbers are proof that—
Ugh. All wrong. This is all wrong!

With the results of these graphs, it's easy to see that the fool-hardy direction that—

"No!" Sal snapped, angrily deleting the words he'd typed out. He'd been at it ever since he had woken up, and he still didn't have a conclusive clincher to his budget proposal. He didn't understand how Solomon was so good at it. His emails and presentations just *flowed*, like water in a brook, and sometimes Sal found himself nodding along despite himself. And for the life of him, he couldn't figure out how to replicate that. His hands felt too big for the keyboard, and he just felt so *incompetent*.

Slamming his hands on the desk, he stood up and went to his window, trying to tell himself that getting worked up over things wasn't going to get him anywhere. He didn't have much success, but he didn't have that much time to try before a knock sounded on his door.

...that was weird. If his brothers ever needed to talk to each other, they usually just texted.

Crossing the room, he opened the heavy wood to see his mother standing there, looking pleased. His temper settled pretty quickly; anything that made his mom happy had to be pretty good news.

"Hi, Mom," he said, hoping she hadn't heard him slam his hands on the desk. That wasn't exactly respectful behavior.

"You have a visitor."

"A what?"

"A visitor, love. Now come to the front door. It's not polite to leave a guest waiting."

Sal's eyebrows shot up, but his mother's happy sort of mood had him curious, so he headed down to the foyer.

And just about the last thing he ever expected was to see Nova waiting there for him.

For a split second, he didn't even recognize the tall woman. She looked *real* different out of her work uniform, dressed in a loose T-shirt and shorts that ended a couple of inches above her knees—one of which definitely looked like it was still puffy and bruised.

It was so different from her jumpsuit that he found himself stalling out a moment as he was going down the stairs. It wasn't like her uniform completely hid her figure, but it was very clear that it was disguising at least *some* of it considering how she looked in those simple shorts.

"Hey there," he said once he was on the landing.

To his surprise, she all but shoved a basket into his face. *"Thank-you-for-helping-me-out!"*

"I—what—oh, you're welcome." He went through a whole spectrum of emotions as he took the basket from her, revealing a good number of cookies and cupcakes sitting inside. They were artfully arranged, and he felt even more confused than ever.

"Oh, did you make those yourself?" his mom asked.

Sal looked overhead to see his mother standing at the top of the stairs. Her cheeks were pink and her eyes were glinting in that way they did whenever she had a real mom idea.

"Oh, yes. I wanted to thank your son for helping me when I got hurt." Nova's eyes went wide. "It wasn't serious, of course. I'm fine. I just wanted to show my gratitude or something along those lines."

But it was clear that his mom wasn't even listening as she rushed down the stairs. Well, she did the closest thing to rushing as a woman in her fifties did when it came to descending anything. "Oh, these look just lovely!" she said once she was close enough. "Sal, may I see the basket?"

"Of course." He handed it off to her, glad for the reprieve. What was it about Nova that made him feel so off-balance? First, she was tackling him, then dismissing him, then breaking her knee in front of him, and now she was baking him *cookies*?

"Goodness, look at this frosting! And these cookies are so cute! You have a gift."

"Oh, I don't know about that," Nova said.

Sal wasn't going to lie; it was actually pretty satisfying to watch a blush slowly creep up Nova's cheeks.

Nova continued, "Anyway, thank you again, I'll be going now."

Before either of them could say a word, the woman practically sprinted out, disappearing down the front steps before the door even had time to close. That was pretty amusing, and Sal found himself smiling as he inspected the basket.

It was cute, as it turned out. Made of wicker, the basket had been polished and painted with delicate, scrolling vines. It was also chock-full of baked goods, delicious-looking cookies, and individually iced cupcakes.

"Can I try one, honey?" Mom asked, looking at him like it was suddenly Christmas.

"Of course," he answered, probably too quickly. But lately his mom only seemed happy when she was with his older brothers and their partners, so it felt good that he could make her smile. Even if it was because of cookies that someone else gave him.

His mother took one of the cupcakes and nearly bit off half of it in one go. Sal laughed, wiping the icing off her nose with a finger. "You're making a mess, Mom."

"*Ith dewisush!*" she said around her mouthful, eyes going wide. She gestured for Sal to try and, despite the fact that he hadn't gotten a single workout in during the past two days, he picked one up and bit into it as well.

The sweetness of it slid over his tongue, but there was a bright, almost citrus taste to it, stopping it just short of being tooth-achingly sugary. It was moist, but held together in his hand, and none of it seemed cloying or stodgy. All in all, it was one of the best cupcakes that Sal had had in a long while.

"Wow, that is something," he said after his bite, his mother still eagerly tearing at the one she took. "But this is way too much for one person to eat. Think if I leave them in the kitchen, everyone else will have a go at them?"

"I don't see how they could resist!" his mom said before a

bright expression crossed her face. "That girl! Who was she? You seemed like you knew her."

"She's one of our new hires. A vet tech or assistant or something."

"Ah! I see! Do you think that maybe I could borrow her for the next wave of baked goods I'm supposed to make for the food pantry?"

"You mean the one that Solomon is running?"

There was some drama that had gone down with the church his family had helped rebuild—Sal hadn't exactly been paying the closest attention—but the result was that his second eldest sibling was in charge of the entire project.

"Yes! And the community center too. Silas and Teddy told me that some of the kids specifically visit after school to see if I've brought them treats. It tickles me pink, to have little tummies all eager for my baking again." She gave him a sort of side-long look, which was impressive considering that she was facing him. Moms were talented that way. "Of course, one of you could always give me some *grandbabies* to spoil—"

"You were talking about baking, Mom?" Sal cut in quickly. That was about the last road he wanted to go down at the moment. What was it about mothers that made them all starry-eyed for their children to have children?

"Oh! Right! Anyway, on that lovely young lady's next shift, please ask if she'd be willing to work in the kitchen with me for a couple of shifts. And the vet too, I suppose."

Sal was surprised when a lick of jealousy flickered through his chest. "You know, *I* can help you in the kitchen."

"That's brilliant, love! Having both you and that sweet young lady will be a huge help. I'll send you an invite for your calendar. Silas just showed me how to use it on my phone, so I figure I better practice so I don't forget!"

She took another cupcake and three cookies before practically floating back to his parent's wing, no doubt to give Dad some of the goodies. Sal watched her go, happy that she was clearly happy, but something else entirely twisting in his stomach.

Approximately zero of that had worked out how he had hoped.

13

Nova

"*Now* come on, love, this'll make you and your friends feel a whole lot better," Nova said, gently petting the side of the young calf's head. He made a disagreeing grunt, his hind legs kicking up for just a minute.

"Aw, come on now. Periwinkle and Runt let me do it without a fuss. You don't want to be a drama queen, do you? Think of what your friends will say!"

Maybe it was silly, but Nova liked to talk to the animals like they understood her. She figured that, even if they didn't, they knew tone and volume well enough that they might be comforted by pleasant chit-chat. But it seemed that the calf in front of her wasn't going to be soothed by some friendly conversation.

Time for the big guns, apparently.

Wrapping one arm around its neck, she took the nose tag

she had ready and curled it through in one quick motion. The calf let out a bleat of alarm, but the thing was in place before the sound even finished.

"There you go! That's not so bad, is it?"

Indigo the calf licked at it, giving her a reproachful look. Whoops, it was probably going to take time to get that trust back.

"Look, it wouldn't have come to this if you didn't insist on chewing on everybody's tails."

That was the thing about cows, and young cows especially, they loved to chew. Which was great when it came to breaking down food for their three stomachs. Less awesome when it came to chewing each other's ears, tails, or even gnawing off whole udders from their mothers and aunts.

Nova shuddered at that. Elizabeth had shown her pictures of damaged utters and her go-to methodology for treating such injuries, which were... not great to look at. As far as Nova was concerned, the best measures were preventive, and the best preventive measure was plastic nose tags.

"Hey there."

Nova let out a short cry and jumped, her knee protesting with a sharp jolt of hot lightning up her thigh. Whirling, she saw none other than Sal there, wearing a white athletic shirt that was about two times too small and casual looking joggers.

"Hello?"

They hadn't spoken since her baked goods hit-and-run a few days earlier, and she'd finally breathed a sigh of relief that all the dust seemed to be settled and they could go back to their everyday lives. Seeing Sal in front of her again was making her nerves spike. What did he want?

"Hey, I have a question but feel free to say no—this isn't compulsory or anything—my mom was wondering if you would be willing to help her out with the upcoming baking this Thursday and Friday so she can deliver it into the city on the weekend. It's for some food pantries and charity stuff. You would be paid, of course. It would be a regular workday for you, but, uh, in the kitchen instead of with the animals."

It was strange to see him jilted and uneven after how smoothly he had handled her when she'd been stuck in the mud in the rain, but it made her feel better that he got flustered too. Like she wasn't a complete and total dork.

"Really? Your mom wants me to help her bake?"

"Yeah, she was real impressed with those cupcakes of yours. Cookies too, judging by how fast they vanished, but I didn't see that one in person."

"Your mom liked my cupcakes?" Nova repeated as if she hadn't heard right. Because she couldn't have heard right. Mrs. Miller, the wife of *the* Mr. McLintoc Miller, liked her cupcakes?

"Practically inhaled one right in front of me."

Huh. Wasn't that something?

Nova nodded. "Sure, why not? I like helping people out. If your mum doesn't think I'd just be in the way, I'm game."

"Considering that she sent me on a mission specifically to recruit you, I doubt she'll think that at all."

"Wow, that's going to go straight to my ego."

"Not sure you really needed that."

She let out a short laugh and that seemed to surprise both of them. "Fair enough. I'm sure seeing her bake will put me right in my place."

"Hey, everything okay over there?"

Nova looked over her shoulder to see Elizabeth standing at the far side of the calf pens, dropping off a box that had to be more nose tags. Her tone wasn't one of concern over seeing Sal, or at least it didn't sound that way to Nova, but the same professionally crisp tone that the vet always had when it came to animal care.

"I'm about a third done!" Nova called back. "No one's having a huge temper tantrum, but Indigo had an attitude."

"Alright, good work. I'll check back later; I think one of the horses might have a case of rain rot and I want to catch it early."

"Yikes, rain rot? How do you think that happened?"

Elizabeth shrugged. "I aim to find out. Oh, also, the twins are out on a walk with their horses. If they swing by, tell them to park their mounts at the spare stable, would you? They've been terrible about answering their phones the past couple of days."

"Right!"

Elizabeth gave a polite nod to the two of them then headed back the way she came, disappearing into her own golf cart.

Nova turned back to Sal, almost having forgotten that he was right there. He was standing with his arms crossed, emphasizing his chest, and Nova forced her eyes up to his face. She was not going to ogle her boss right to his face.

...although technically she supposed she shouldn't be ogling him period. Whatever. She was only human.

"What exactly are you doing here?" he asked haltingly, like he was trying to find a conversation topic but had accidentally switched to a new language midway.

She held up a plastic tag, and when no recognition flashed across his eyes, she gave him a skeptical look. "What kind of cowboy doesn't know what a nose tag is?"

"A nose what?" he shot right back, sounding more comfortable. "And I'm not a cowboy."

"You sure do look like a cowboy to me," Nova said, her eyes flicking down to his nice boots. "You live on a ranch. Your last name is Miller. What's that one American phrase? Oh right, if it looks like a duck, walks like a duck and quacks like a duck, chances are it's probably a duck."

"That's not really how it goes."

Nova just waved her hand. "The intent is there. You know what I mean."

He smiled, shaking his head, and finally he looked less like he was going to panic and run for it at any second. If Nova wasn't still so busy trying to figure him out, she might have been flattered that he was so flustered by her, but it just made everything that much more confusing. Was Sal secretly a twin too, and there was a confident, jerky one then a shy, stilted one who talked about baking? Seemed more plausible.

"Do I?"

"Aw come on now, you keep playin' pedantic with me and I'll think you're one of those rhinestone cowboys."

The look he gave her was far more endearing than it had any right to be. "A what now?"

"You heard me. A rhinestone cowboy. Someone who's all dolled up for the role but too shiny and rich to actually do anything useful."

"You calling me pretty?"

She leveled him with a *look*. "What, are compliments so dried up around you that you have to go fishing for them now?"

He chuckled, a low, rumbling sound that seemed to slide along her skin before reaching her ears, leaving goose bumps along their path. Her heart skipped a beat and she did her best to cover her slightly hitched breath with a cough.

"Well, I guess I ain't much of a cowboy in any respect, rhinestone or not," Sal answered after a beat.

There was a sort of earnestness to his statement that Nova

hadn't expected. Sure, they had just been bantering back and forth, but she was pretty sure that he'd transitioned right to being serious.

He continued, "I've never been much for ranch life except riding and teaching my horse tricks. Past five years or so, seems I've gotten away from even that."

Several thoughts flashed through Nova's mind all at once, and all of them were completely hilarious. First of all, the thought of a massive Sal riding atop a horse was pretty comical. He had to have a truly *gargantuan* mount.

Then there was the image of the massive Sal teaching his gargantuan mount *tricks*. It was impossible and fascinating at the same time.

But then there was also another thought, quieter and dripped in melancholy. It was clear that there was tension between Sal and his brothers, and she couldn't help but wonder if a good chunk of it was from the young man not fitting in anywhere. Solomon was clearly all about the finances of the ranch and expanding their charitable enterprise. Silas and Sterling both seemed pretty into improving their animal's lives as well as community outreach. Nova was pretty sure she'd heard something about a soil experiment too? Though she wasn't sure about that one.

But if Sal wasn't really into ranch life... where did that leave him?

"You... taught your horses tricks?"

"Why do you say it like you're so surprised?" he retorted, quick as anything. There was the confident side of him, coming out again.

"I mean, to be perfectly honest, I'm surprised that you've managed to house an elephant here without me noticing it."

"An elephant?"

"Sure, that's about the only creature I can imagine you riding without damaging a poor creature's spine."

"Oh har-har, you're hilarious."

"But seriously, what tricks did you teach your horse?" She didn't know why she was so caught on the idea, but it was definitely jarring to imagine the juggernaut in front of her doing loops or jumps on a stallion's back.

"Ah, nothing that impressive."

There was a soft laugh from just beyond the pens as the twins rounded the barn, walking their horses. "Don't let Sal fool you. In his high school days, Sal used to run a lot with the show circuit," Sterling said.

"Did all sorts of feats. Difficult stuff. Stuff that made Mom cover her eyes," Silas added with a chuckle. The brothers certainly had uncanny timing.

"Wait, is that true?" Nova asked, knowing her eyes were wide and not even caring. "You were doing shows?"

"They make it sound more exciting than it was."

Oh geez. He wasn't even *trying* to deny it! Salvatore Miller, the giant with muscles the size of her head, once did horse tricks for pony shows and rodeos. Holy halibut.

"I... You... why did you ever stop?"

But Sal shrugged, a faint color atop his cheeks. "Just one of those things."

"You didn't like it?"

"No, I did."

"Liked it?" Silas called as he and his twin rounded another corner by the end of the pens, the one that would lead them to the stables. Oh right, she was supposed to warn them about that. "He loved it."

"Hey, Elizabeth said to take your mounts over to the spare stable. She mentioned she tried to call but you didn't answer.

She thinks there might be a case of rain rot with one of them."

"Rain rot? That's not good."

"That's what I said."

"Alright, thanks, Nova. I forgot my phone in the house," Sterling called, and then they were disappearing from sight between some pieces of equipment.

"So you loved it," Nova affirmed, studying the man in front of her and trying to picture all of it. What did he look like in high school? Was he always a jacked lad, or had he grown into his form? It was hard to imagine him as anything other than ripped, but she was pretty certain that he hadn't popped out of the womb with a six-pack.

"I was enthusiastic about it."

"If you loved it, then why did you quit?"

Another shrug. "I couldn't really find a reason to justify it."

What? None of that made sense. "Isn't loving it enough of a reason?"

He just blinked at her, like she'd really started talking in another language. When it became clear that he didn't have a response to that, she cleared her throat.

"Uh, anyway, I better get back to work," she said.

"Can I help you?"

His words came almost too quickly after her own statement, all mushed together in one breath. "Come again?"

"The, uh, tags. You want help? I could. Could help, that is. If you want."

She gave him an appraising sort of once over, but the expression on his face did seem genuine, if not a tad nervous. "You're probably going to get that nice, clean outfit right messy."

"It can be washed."

"Alright then, if you don't mind it, I don't mind showing you what to do. I figure you'll be real good at holding the squirmy ones."

The smile that broke across his face was truly something else. It made him look younger, unguarded. It was suddenly much easier to imagine him teaching a mount how to canter or barrel run.

"Alright, what can I do?"

She showed him and he listened. Really listened, not half-listened like so many people did when she tried to explain things to them. Namely, her family. They always seemed to think that she was incompetent, and Nova couldn't help but feel like they were patronizing her more often than not.

The task began to fly by. Not that it was difficult before, but it sure was a lot easier with another set of hands. Especially when those hands were as large and as capable as Sal's were. For not being much of one for ranch life, the calves all seemed to like him plenty, some of them even gracing his face with licks. And of course, it wouldn't be a weekday if Gwendolyn didn't try to eat his hair. But Sal handled it like a champ, laughing and changing his grip so that the girl couldn't give him an impromptu bald spot. Nova wished she could have met this Sal first. Maybe everything would have been a lot different if their initial interaction hadn't been her trying to stop him from killing an innocent snake.

Oh well, what was done was done, and there was only moving forward.

"You're pretty good at this, you know," she said when they were almost done, trying to sound nonchalant. She had a theory in the back of her head and she wanted to test it out.

"Am I?" He grinned again, his cheeks coloring slightly.

"Yup. Wouldn't have known this was your first time."

"Thanks."

There it was: more pink spreading across his cheeks. How often did anyone compliment the guy on something that wasn't his looks? Did his brothers say anything nice about his abilities, whatever they were? Did his father? It seemed unlikely, especially judging by how Sal had quit a hobby he'd been into because... she actually wasn't sure about why. Was it not "profitable"? What did "not being able to justify it" mean? She didn't have a clue.

"Keep on going, and I just might kidnap you from the house to help with all my grunt work," Nova said.

"Is that so?"

"Oh yeah, totally."

"You know, I am one of your bosses."

"Yeah, yeah, help me get a hold of Persephone. She's a drama queen too."

He tsked at her jokingly but did as she asked. They fell into a sort of rhythm, and Nova enjoyed the company. She'd gotten so used to being on her own for the past few years that she had kind of forgotten what it was like to have companionship for a few hours. Sure, she worked with Elizabeth plenty, and while the veterinarian was nice, that wasn't exactly what Nova would call quality hang-out time.

An hour passed, maybe a touch more, and then they were all done. Nova was almost remiss about it. She couldn't remember the last time she had talked to a human at such length. And she really had done most of the talking. Sure, Sal answered and quipped with her, but he didn't start most of their conversation in the calves' pen, like he was still finding his footing.

"Look at that, we're done pretty early. Thanks again, mate. You helped quite a lot."

"I'm glad I could. I'll see you this Thursday at ten a.m. at the manor?"

Oh right. She was going to have to be in close quarters with *the* Mrs. Miller in their fancy mansion. Yikes. "I'll be there, alright."

"Good."

He gave her a quick nod then headed off, vaulting over the side of the pen when he neared it. For being a real big guy, he could really *move*.

Nova shook her head, stopping herself from biting her lip like some sort of thirsty mess. He was her *boss*. Besides, she hadn't dated anyone since high school. Some things just weren't her scene.

Taking a deep breath, she wiped off her hands and went to find Elizabeth. Maybe a little hard labor would help clear her mind of exactly what it wanted to linger on.

14

Salvatore

*S*al was nervous. He could feel it radiating from his brain down into his hands, which trembled slightly if he wasn't gripping something, and then to his feet, which were sweating something fierce in his house slippers. His stomach was doing that vaguely nauseous sloshing thing it did whenever his anxiety got too high. The urge to go lift heavy objects until it passed was racing through Sal's mind.

Because he was nervous about *baking*.

It was utterly ridiculous, but as he stood in the kitchen hauling down items his mother needed from their tall cabinets, he couldn't help but feel like he was a bull in the china shop. Oh geez, his hands were beginning to sweat too. He was doomed.

There was a knock at the front door and all that sweat turned cold as one of their staff answered. That *had* to be Nova.

She was in the manor. She was in the manor and soon she was going to be in the kitchen, and he was going to have to bake with her for *hours*.

He should have thought through the whole situation a lot more.

Except it hadn't really seemed like *that* big of a deal until the time with the nose tags thing. Sure, she always threw him off and made him feel... perplexed, but something had shifted since their time in the pens a couple of days earlier.

She'd been nice to him. And not in an overly sweet, cloying way that some folks like to fawn over him. There hadn't been that appreciative glint in her eye like a woman sizing him up for amorous reasons either. No, she'd teased him like they were equals, then complimented him when he did a good job. And he believed her too. Something about Nova made her seem like the last person who would patronize him or say something that she didn't mean.

And what she'd said about trick riding stuck with him. He'd quit because it hadn't really been all that respectable. His father had said multiple times that trick riding was for cowgirls who couldn't handle the important tasks of ranching and had rarely come to shows. Sal remembered being told by some of his other rich friends that it was a waste of money, that it made the other men in Dad's circle insinuate that Sal was some sort of fop and that McLintoc Miller had a soft hand. That was right about when he stopped and threw himself entirely into building as much muscle as he could. His teenage self promised that he'd show them who was a fop!

In the back of his mind, he knew it didn't work that way. Muscles weren't an indicator of a man's worth. But that mean, biting voice kept telling him that he had to be big enough to prove his manliness anyway. It was exhausting.

"Hello there," Nova said, her escort bringing her to the kitchen before giving a polite head tilt and exiting. "I hope I'm not late."

Sal checked his watch. It was ten minutes before ten. Hardly late.

"Not at all, darling!" Mom said, flittering away from where she'd been standing beside Sal to rush over and throw her arms about Nova in a hug. The young woman certainly seemed surprised by the action, stiffening slightly, before relaxing and accepting the hug. Good, Sal wouldn't abide anyone who brushed off his mother. "How are you? Did you have a good morning?"

"I did have a good morning. I've been excited and I'll admit a little nervous about coming to help you bake."

"Well, thank you so much again for agreeing to help me. When Sal told me that you agreed, I just about passed out from relief. Those cupcakes were probably the best cupcakes I've ever had."

"I'm honored that you want me to help. Is there that much on the to-do list?"

"Well, I want to make some plain loaves, some dessert ones, cinnamon rolls, lemon squares, key lime pie and of course cookies, cupcakes and some other smaller cakes. It's a lot for one person, although I have managed before."

Yeah, she really had. Sal remembered those times, Mom baking up a storm in the kitchen while the help tried to clean up and assist however she needed. But Mrs. Miller had always been the queen of the kitchen, and their hired staff was mostly for cleaning, laundry, and the like. Not entirely skills that were useful in the kitchen. And considering that Solomon had increased their pay and reduced their hours, it wasn't like those particular employees were around all too often.

"That's right impressive! Just tell me where you need me, and I'll get started. I really am only a novice at this, mind you."

"Goodness! I just love that accent of yours. It's so pretty! Where are you from, sweetheart?"

"North Yorkshire, on the Air Force base there. My family's settled just south of Liverpool now."

"Lovely. I have always adored British accents. I bet we sound pretty funny to you."

"Not really. I think most of you sound real nice. Warm-like."

Mom made an approving sound that almost sounded like a swoon. Abruptly, Sal was starting to get why all of his brother's lady friends tended to visit the house so much. Clearly his mother was different with them than she was with all of her boys, all bright smiles and unchecked enthusiasm. Come to think of it, Mom didn't really have that many female friends. He remembered her having some when he was younger, but those all faded, his mother saying something about social ladder-climbing and false friends. Maybe she was starved for feminine energy.

That thought made him frown. He hated the thought of his mom being lonely or wanting for something. She was, in his opinion, one of the most loving women in the world. She had dealt with raising six unruly boys to adulthood and was now having to face the changing dynamics of her family. If he could, he would wrap her in bubble wrap and make sure that nothing ever upset her again.

Unfortunately, the world didn't work that way.

"Now if that isn't the sweetest thing! You are a gem, my dear. Now, why don't you go wash your hands in that small sink on the corner of the kitchen island and grab yourself an apron. The longer ones are in the back from when my boys used to occasionally help me when they were younger. You're one of those tall drinks of water, so you'll be wanting to use one of those."

Nova dipped her head, blushing, and if that wasn't a look that Sal's brain definitely took notice of. "Thank you, ma'am."

"Oh please, none of that. You can call me Mom or Mama Miller. Ma'am is what strangers call me, and there are no strangers in my kitchen."

"Yes, ma—I mean, Mum Miller."

"Mum Miller! Did you hear that, Sal?" Mom turned to him, a wide smile on her face. "Mum Miller, how fancy! I feel even more elegant as we speak."

"Careful, Mom, keep being over-the-top and Nova might tease us about our own colloquialisms."

"Colloquialisms? What a word. You always have been such a smart boy." His mom walked over to him, surprising him with a kiss on the cheek. She thought he was smart? But Solomon, Silas, and Simon were the smart ones. Or at least... that was what Sal had always thought. "And Nova, is that your name, sweetheart?"

"Yeah." Sal could tell that the British woman was nervous judging by her response, and he was glad he wasn't the only one. Granted, Mom being so lively was certainly helping him loosen up. It was hard to feel bad when she was so clearly enthused. He couldn't remember the last time he'd seen her so happy and bouncy.

Ah, when Solomon had gotten her that pretty, lilac, pink, and mint golf cart that she practically drove everywhere. Mom loved that thing more than her own minivan. Especially considering the minivan hadn't been out of the garage in over a year while he saw her joyriding with the Frenchie girl a couple weeks earlier.

"Goodness, what a name! A star full of dazzling light! I've seen pictures of those in Nat Geo, you know. Always so stunning. It suits you though."

Now Nova's cheeks were a bright red. "I don't know about that, ma'am—Mum Miller."

"Well, I do! Anyway, before I lose more time with my talking, I should explain that in my house we do our measurements via weight rather than cups and the like. I find it goes faster for large-batch baking. You and Sal will be on the scales I have at first, measuring for the recipes I printed out, and then eventually I'll pull you onto mixing duty. Sound fun?"

"Sounds fun," Nova agreed with a smile, going around to the longer side of the island where six different scales of various sizes had been arranged, all with pieces of paper next to them and two bowls behind them, one labeled wet and the other labeled dry.

"You go and join her now, Sal, I think you've gotten down everything I need, and I always have my step stool. Nova, would you be a darling and answer any questions he might have? Sal used to help me in the kitchen and knows the basics, but some of the things we're doing today are more complex."

"Right, no problem here," Nova said, giving his Mom a salute. And as the older woman turned her back, Nova sent a wink to him. And oh, if that wink didn't have his heart reacting far more than it should. Were her eyelashes always that thick? Or was he just really noticing how pretty her deep umber eyes were?

Uh-oh.

"Alright, you ready to do some measuring?" Nova asked.

"Sure," he answered stiffly, tongue thick.

"Perfect. Now the first thing is... uh, where are all the ingredients?"

Without a word, he reached for the hanging cabinet above the kitchen island, the one that was right smack dab in the middle of the rack for hooking pots and pans onto, opening the sliding door to reveal where they'd placed the flour, sugar, baking soda, baking powder—apparently those were two entirely different things??? Baking was confusing—seasonings and other ingredients.

"The eggs, milk, and lemon juice are still in the fridge. I figured I'd pull them out when we got to that."

"Great. I just need a pitcher of lukewarm water then if you could grab that and fill it in the corner sink."

And just like that, they fell easily into the start of things, Mom bustling on the other side of the kitchen with all of her prep. Sal had never been bad at directions, per se, but he did hate when folks condescended him or treated him like he wasn't smart enough. But Nova never once sounded like that. In fact, she made it almost kind of fun. Like they were a couple of friends completing a new and exciting project together. She didn't make him feel incompetent. She didn't make him feel *small.*

It was nice.

"Goodness, I have to say, Mum Miller, I'm right glad you're using grams right now. It makes it easier for my mind."

Mom paused from where she was lining a pan with something, maybe a stick of butter? "I didn't even think about that! You're a metric gal, aren't you?"

"Both, actually. Living on military bases for a while and being homeschooled there got me started on the American system, but then I went to secondary school off-base, and I got used to using metric. It does make the math a right bit easier."

"Secondary school is what again?" Sal asked, trying to recall if that was elementary or middle school. He wished the whole world would just agree on the same terms. Would certainly make things simpler.

"Oh, right. High school, basically."

"So, you were homeschooled for a while?" Mom asked, sounding interested even as her hands kept moving and she was on to doing something else.

"Yeah, it made all the moving around easier. Being an army brat and all."

"You didn't just live in, uh... Northern York..."

"North Yorkshire," Nova corrected with a charming smile.

And for some reason, Sal's mind piped up that he knew this answer and he should show off to the woman beside him that he listened to what she said.

"She lived all over. Guam and Japan and some other places before her family ended up in the UK." He tried to say it casually, but he wasn't sure how much he succeeded.

"Wow! So well-traveled! I have to admit, I'm jealous. I've always wanted to go to Japan and Europe, but somehow, I've never found the time. Raising six boys will do that to you, I suppose."

"Traveling is much more fun than repeat moving. I hardly remember most of those places."

Sal could tell by the way Nova's words hit his hearing that she had her head turned towards him, and when he took a glance at her, she looked pretty impressed.

"You remembered all that?" she asked more quietly than her responses to Mom.

"I remember almost everything you tell me."

"Huh."

"Maybe next year I can convince your father to relax for a moment and take me on a trip! Simon is doing it now; I'm sure he'll have plenty of recommendations."

As if he had been magically summoned, the front door slammed open and Dad's angry voice drifted down the hall into the kitchen through its open door.

Sal couldn't make out exactly what he was saying, but the tone was *very* apparent. There was a measured sort of response that sounded like it could be Solomon, but their response was much quieter.

The warm, happy nature of the kitchen quickly shifted with all three of its occupants halting what they were doing. None of them said anything, but Sal felt embarrassment boil in his stomach.

Why then? Why did it have to be when Nova was right next to him? While everything felt so natural and pleasant. Why did his brothers have to ruin everything?

A quick glance at Nova revealed her expression was definitely shocked and mildly horrified. And both of those aspects only continued as Dad's voice grew louder. How it got louder when it was clear he was retreating back to his wing of the house, Sal didn't know, but that was definitely what was happening.

It seemed an eternity before the voice mostly faded, a dull roar somewhere rooms away, but Sal felt like everything was still happening at once. He knew he should probably go after his father to see what was up, to provide back up in case Solomon, Silas or Sterling were trying to push something else on him. But he also wanted to stay and try to play it off to Nova. For a reason he couldn't name, he didn't want her to think that they were mean or uncivilized. Even if his father had sounded *really* angry.

"Why don't you go ahead and shut the door, Sal dear?" Mom asked, her mouth drawn into a tight line. "I feel a draft in here."

There was a beat where he didn't answer, his gaze sliding from his mom to the door. He knew that if he wanted to improve himself in his father's graces, if he wanted to show that he was a leader and take over Solomon's tenuous position as primary heir, then he needed to go to his father's office and back him up. Prove his worth.

"Sal? Would you be a dear?"

It was his chance. A strategic move if there ever was. Maybe it would even be the turning point where McLintoc Miller would finally see that Sal really was trying.

Nodding, Sal moved from his spot at the scales, walking to the exit. With one last look to the hallway that led out to the foyer, he quietly shut the door.

15

Nova

"So, I've just finished kneading the bread. Nova, would you be a dear and place these in the proving cabinet for me?"

"You have a proving cabinet?" Nova asked, wiping her hands on her apron and crossing over to the bowl filled with a perfectly round lump of dough. Mrs. Miller was not kidding about her baking expertise.

"Of course. It's the only way I'd have a hope of finishing all this in time!"

"What's a proving cabinet?" Sal asked, setting down the scoop he'd been using to pour into the small bowl on his scale.

Nova hadn't missed how he'd almost dropped the flour when she'd spoken, he'd been concentrating so hard on preparing the dry mix from his mom's summertime cake recipe.

"It's something used to help the yeast in the bread activate," Nova said helpfully. "It can be warmed but at much lower temperatures than the oven can. Too hot and you kill all the yeast and there's no leavening, you see? And uh... there's something else, isn't there?"

"It has controlled humidity," Mum Miller said with a smile. "But otherwise, you are correct."

"Oh," Sal said, his gaze flicking to Nova. "Show me how to use it?"

"Sure," Nova answered, flashing him a smile. It had been a couple hours since the whole incident with his father, and while that had certainly been uncomfortable, he'd seemed to relax since.

Funny, Nova had been so sure that he was going to rush out when it happened, drawn into another family fight. But nope, he'd closed the door and picked up right where they'd left off before the row.

"Are these standard bread settings, Mum Miller?"

"You've got it, sweetie."

Normally Nova wasn't much for pet names, but there was something sweet about the older woman that made them alright. They weren't condescending or anything like that. Just cute little nicknames from someone who was about as warm and shiny as the sun shining in from the large windows.

"Okay, so these knobs here are how you control it. First though, you want to make sure your bread is covered when you put it in."

Sal nodded along, giving her hands a studious look as he observed her every step. It made Nova feel so... *respected.* Like they were equals and she had useful information to give him. It wasn't exactly a feeling she was used to, and she found herself flushing as they returned to their scales.

"I think you two have gotten plenty ahead. Nova, how are you at mixing icing?" Mrs. Miller asked.

"What kind of icing?"

"I'm debating between cream cheese and buttercream."

"As long as it's not royal icing, I'm game."

Mrs. Miller wrinkled her nose. "Royal icing is for people who want to have overly fancy treats over tasty ones. I hate the texture of it."

"Me too!" Nova said excitedly. "My whole family goes nuts for biscuits with that kind of decoration, but I find it gritty."

"Biscuits?" Sal asked from behind her.

"Sorry, cookies," Nova corrected. "I haven't messed that one up in ages."

Mrs. Miller chuckled. "A woman after my own heart. Well, I have a batch of cookies and another of cupcakes about to come out in five minutes. They'll need to cool, so why don't you hop on the cream cheese batch, and I'll mix the buttercream. Do you need the recipe? I just follow a standard one, with a lil' vanilla and lemon juice added."

"That sounds good. I remember the portions."

"Ah! Perfect, where have you been all my life! I always secretly hoped that one of my sons would be more culinarily inclined, but most of them only humor me."

"Hey, I like baking with you," Sal said, jokingly miffed from where he was still measuring.

Nova thought he looked much cuter than someone his size and shape had any right to. There was flour across one of his cheeks, his hair was mussed, and his tongue was sitting out of the side of his mouth as he very carefully poured more flour onto the bowl atop his scale. He was just so sweet. How had she never noticed that before?

"I just got kinda big for the kitchen," Sal continued.

"That's true. He went through that typical teenage awkward phase where his limbs were all too big for him. Kept stepping on my feet."

"And breaking things."

"The good thing is that you've grown into yourself, haven't you?" Mrs. Miller blew him a kiss and he just laughed, shaking his head.

If Nova didn't know better, she would think they were a normal family. How did they go from this loving, wonderful, and homey sort of reaction to the tension she had witnessed between Sal and his brothers?

Was it money? She was willing to bet it was money. If there was one thing she'd noticed since coming to the States, it was that there were a whole lot of people who worshipped at the altar of money rather than God's. Whether it was putting a price on human life, medical treatment, or schooling, it definitely seemed like dollar bills ruled all in the good ol' U.S.A. There were lovely people, of course, like Auntie Kini, and the older man who sold flowers down her block, not to mention Elizabeth and dozens of others, but they seemed to be the minority so many times.

Nova didn't get it. Jesus had mentioned time and time again how the rich weren't likely to get into heaven and how the lust for gain was the quickest path to darkness, but that seemed to be glossed over. Especially with gross megachurches and pastors who were millionaires. If there ever was an oxymoron, it was right there.

"Yeah, grown is an understatement," Nova teased.

"I have no idea what you're talking about," Mum Miller said with the same wit her son had. "My little boy is clearly perfect."

"Not little, not a boy, and most certainly not perfect." Sal shook his head again and went to the fridge. "Oh, Mom, we're out of eggs."

"Shoot! I forgot to move them in from the pantry's fridge. Would you go grab about two dozen for me? I think that's all we'll need for today."

"Wait... you have another fridge... in your pantry?" Nova asked.

"Of course. Where else would we put the overflow items? It's much more cost-efficient to buy in bulk, after all."

Yup. It was definitely money.

"Right," Nova said.

"Anything else you need from there?" Sal asked.

"You know what? How about a box of butter and then a bottle of that sparkling apple cider. I think we've all earned a treat."

"Breaking out the apple cider already? You must be feeling happy."

"Well, we're about three hours ahead on my list, thanks to the two of you. I don't see why I wouldn't be happy!"

Sal nodded and headed out of a door in the back of the kitchen past his mother, leaving Nova alone with the kind lady.

Although she had been nothing but nice, Nova felt that rise of apprehension in her. She never knew how to act with parents and when Sal was there, she'd had a buffer. But being alone with a millionaire mother? ...or was it billionaire mother? Yeah, Nova was pretty sure it was the "B" one. Well, it was making her nerves rise up again.

"You and Sal seem to get along," Mrs. Miller remarked idly as she unwrapped several sticks of butter.

But Nova knew better than that. That was an investigatory mother question if she ever heard one. "Do we?"

"Of course. It's not often I ever see him interact with employees. I do love my boy, but he tends to be somewhat standoffish."

"Does he?" She was probably playing it too careful, but she suddenly felt like she was walking on some sort of tightrope she hadn't been prepared for.

But if Mum Miller noticed, she didn't point it out. "Then again, I suppose all of my boys kind of ended up going through that stage. They didn't use to be like that, though, not when they were younger."

"What happened?"

Mrs. Miller frowned down into her bowl as she opened another cabinet to reveal even more flour, sugar, and other baking things. Nova didn't want to think how expensive it was to have double of all the ingredients they could possibly need. Not when she was still sticking to forty dollars a week for groceries out of habit.

"Who can say? Maybe it's just getting older? Clint always says that I raised them too soft, that he had to harden them up for the business. Shark-eat-shark world and all that."

"Clint?"

"Mr. Miller, my husband. I love the man, I do. But..."

"But?" Nova asked cautiously. She could sense that she was on ground that needed to be tread across lightly.

But Mum Miller just shook her head. "This isn't really appropriate conversation, my apologies. Would you pass me a sifter from the drawer right by your hip?"

And just like that, the vulnerable state the woman had been in was closed off, just in time too, as Sal came in with his arms full of the items he'd been sent to fetch.

"There's my handsome son. Put those on the counter, would you?" Mrs. Miller said.

He did, and then went back to his measuring, his eyes switching from Nova to his mother. She had the feeling that he knew that *something* had happened but was trying to figure out what.

"Your mother spent the entire time you were gone telling me embarrassing stories about your childhood," Nova said, giving the woman an out. She also didn't miss how Mum Miller's shoulders dropped and she let out a quiet breath.

"Is that so?" Sal asked, his eyebrows rising.

Mrs. Miller turned to him with that brilliant smile back in place, her eyes no longer looking wet or uncertain. Amazing. Did all mothers do that or was it exclusive to the lovely older woman beside her?

"You know how I get to talking. Now, how are you coming along with that cake recipe?"

"Moving on to the wet ingredients. That's why I went to get eggs," Sal said.

"Right, of course. Just make sure you don't add the sugar but set it in one of the small cups to the side."

"Why?"

"Sugar can burn the eggs," Nova supplied, relieved that her diversion tactic worked.

"Wait, sugar can what? That's not true. That can't be true."

"Not literally," Mrs. Miller said, pointing her sifter at the two of them. "Sugar is a hygroscopic substance, which means it absorbs water. Since eggs are comprised of fat, protein, a few natural sugars, and water, it absorbs the liquid through the yolk's membrane, leaving the protein molecules to go all stringy and clump closer together. That's why you get the harder, clumpy bits that are impossible to whisk out."

Nova didn't quite know what to say, staring at the older woman while blinking owlishly. From the corner of her eye, she could see that Sal was equally mystified, which made her feel somewhat better.

"What?" Mrs. Miller asked primly. "I was going to be a nurse before I met your father. So I needed to learn math and chemistry and biology. Did you lot think you get all your smarts from him?"

Sal whistled while Nova couldn't help but crack a smile. "Well, baking is scientific."

"Delicious science. Nursing was one of the few sciences a young married woman was allowed to be interested in back then." Her sifter pointed again. "Never forget how lucky you are, sweetie. If I had the same freedoms you do when I was younger..." A dreamy look crossed her face, but then her eyes landed on Sal and she quickly shook it off. "Never mind that. I wouldn't give up my life now for the world. Not when I've got six wonderful sons and a loving husband."

"Yeah, there are plenty of people who would give up an arm, a leg, and then some for your life," Nova said before she thought better of it. But if either of the Millers thought negatively of her words, they didn't show it, and instead they all busied themselves baking again.

The hours flew by, with the three of them not even taking a break for lunch—although that was probably from all the sweet sampling they were doing. Nova was definitely suffering from a sugar high by the time three o'clock rolled around and Mum Miller sat on a stool with a huff.

"Alright, I think that's good for today. We've covered practically all my counter space. You two head out, and I'll work on packaging things up so we can finish the rest tomorrow."

Nova looked around at the impressive spread they had. Four of the loaves had come out of one of the ovens while the confections were cooling down from their time in the other.

There were already four batches of them frosted and spread out on the area that had started off as the measuring station, which was probably one of the reasons why Nova's wrist was cramping so hard. Holding an icing bag for so long definitely strained muscles she wasn't used to needing. Then there were the cupcakes in the fridge and others in plastic carrying cases, ready to be placed in the car and driven to the city.

"We sure did a lot, didn't we?" Nova said.

"That we did, and I wouldn't have been able to get this much done without the two of you! I'd be up until midnight, at least, and my hands would be screaming. This truly has been a blessing."

"Hey, I'll be a blessing any day if it's for you," Sal said, crossing to his mother and pressing a kiss to the top of her just-graying hair.

"Flatterer!" she objected, although she seemed absolutely pleased as punch. "And Miss Nova, I'll see you tomorrow at ten again? It's the custards and pies, for the most part, tomorrow, so I'll need you more than ever."

"I'll be there, Mum Miller."

"Perfect! Give me a hug then before you go and do whatever it is you young people do."

"Mom, you can't just order people to—"

But Nova was already crossing to her and giving her a warm hug. Nova wasn't the touchiest person, but she wasn't... *not* either, and embracing the kind woman seemed like something she wanted to do. So, she did.

"I'll see you tomorrow," Nova said.

With a quick tip of her head, Nova high-tailed it out of there before she could run into anyone else. Not that she needed to keep her presence a secret, considering she had been invited in by the matriarch herself, but it was just that she didn't want the wonderful mood she was in to be diluted by anything at all. Whether it be family drama, tensions, or whatever it was that was bothering the rich folks around her.

Thankfully, she got to her car without interruption and headed home, smiling the whole way. She hadn't expected to like the whole cooking expedition as much as she had. In fact, "like" didn't seem to be the appropriate word. She'd felt welcomed. At home. Which was bizarre considering the mega-mansion was just about the farthest thing from a home that Nova had ever seen.

But Mrs. Miller was so warm and kind. She'd opened her arms and her kitchen like there was nothing to it. It was so different from how Nova's own mother had acted. Still acted, technically, considering how scathing she was when Nova bothered to call. Could families really be like that?

It didn't seem possible.

But Nova found herself excited to go back again. Maybe the Miller kitchen could be her little slice away from the rest of the world. Goodness knew she didn't mind an escape.

16

Salvatore

Sal washed his face, looking at his reflection in the bathroom mirror. He normally didn't pay much attention to his skin, but he found himself looking out for any pimples or ingrown hairs. When he didn't spot anything, his eyes went to the stubble on his chin. Solomon was the only one of the family that really had the five o'clock shadow going, the twins and Simon usually keeping it clean-shaven. Apparently, Samuel had started growing a beard out at Aunt Annie's house, but Sal hadn't seen that yet.

Maybe he should shave his stubble off? Make sure he was all clean and impressive looking for—

...wait, what was he even doing? Pushing away from the mirror, he denied that he was thinking about shaving just to impress Nova. That was ridiculous.

But then he was turning to the mirror, looking at his face this way and then that. Did the stubble make him look dashing? Like a cowboy? Or did he just look lazy? Dirty?

His mind wandered to what Nova's type could be. She was clearly capable, tough, and outdoorsy. Maybe she'd gotten into ranch life looking for a rustic type to settle down and homestead with her.

Sal looked down at his hands. What had once been calloused and toughened up from all the horse training he had done was now soft and maintained. The most demanding thing his fingers usually had to do anymore was type or grip a steering wheel.

That was depressing.

...maybe a visit to the stables was in order. Get reacquainted with all their mounts. Sal hadn't really had much interest in the horses ever since his good old guy, Midas, had passed.

His phone's alarm went off and he grabbed at it, realizing he only had about a half-hour before Nova arrived, and that was only if she didn't arrive early.

And given what he knew about Nova, she absolutely was going to arrive early.

"What are you doing?" he asked his reflection as he realized how caught up he was. His reflection didn't answer, naturally.

Nova was just helping out his mother, and they all happened to have a good time. That was no reason for his heart to be thumping and for him to feel like it was Christmas.

...except that was exactly how he felt.

His second alarm went off, and he shut that off too while he headed out the door. He wanted to get to the kitchen early and shove some actual food down his gullet before Nova got there. Goodness knew he had about seven thousand calories the day before—and all of them sugary. He needed some actual protein to balance it out.

"Oh, there you are, honey," Mom said, already in the kitchen. She had a different apron on than the day before, which made sense considering how she liked to collect them. "I made some biscuits and gravy if you'd like some."

"Is that even a question?" he retorted happily, crossing to the skillet on the stove. He couldn't remember the last time that his mother had made good old biscuits and gravy. It seemed like a holdover from his high school years. Happier times when things were less complicated. "You didn't have to make anything, you know. Not when you already have so much on your to-do list."

"I don't mind. I was feeling inspired."

"Were you?"

She nodded, taking a truly comically large bite of what was on her plate. Sal helped himself while she chewed, sitting across from her and pouring himself a glass from the pitcher of water between them.

"So..."

He knew that tone. That was a mom-tone if there ever was one. "...so?"

"This young woman, Nova. How do you know her?"

There it was. "She's an employee, Mom. You know that."

"Oh yeah, sure. Sure. But Sterling hired her, and Silas is the one who set up all her paperwork, and then Elizabeth is the one she works under so... how do *you* know her?"

Had his mom found all that out in one night? Sal didn't know whether to be impressed or disturbed. "We ran into each other on the farm."

"Uh-huh."

"That's it, Mom."

"Right. So you ran into her, and then she felt the need to bake you a basket of delicious food and thank you for getting her out of a tough spot." Her eyes narrowed. "Doesn't quite add up, if you ask me."

Sal didn't want to tell her that the only reason he knew Nova was because the young woman had stopped him from killing a snake that was mostly minding its own business. Mom wasn't thrilled about snakes, but the more time that passed, the more Sal cringed at how he had acted. A *shovel*? Really? It wasn't like the critter was in the house.

"Why don't you get to your point, Mom?" Sal tried to ask as lightly as he could.

"Do I have to have a point?"

"Only when you clearly do."

She shrugged, sending him an innocent look while batting her eyes. "I have no idea what you mean. She's a lovely young lady, that's all. I like her. You seem to as well."

"I'm not my brothers." The words were out of his mouth before he could think better of it.

"What do you mean by that?"

"I mean, I'm not going to run into some random woman in a meet-cute and then start dating them. I've got the business to worry about. We're in a difficult spot right now; I'm sure Dad's told you as much."

But Mom just waved her hand as she finished up her plate. "Business, schmizness. The only *business* I care about is having some grandbabies before I return to the dirt."

Sal groaned. "Mom, you're not even that old."

"*That* old? What is that supposed to mean?"

Sal held his hands up. "Hey, you're the one talking about grandbabies!"

She just huffed, although he could tell it was all in good nature. "I had Solomon at the ripe ol' age of twenty! You'd think one of you could do me the courtesy of falling in love and makin' a family for me to spoil rotten."

"See, when you state your intention outright like that, surely you could see how it might hurt your chances of any of that happening?"

"Please, it is my God-given right to fill your children up with sugar and kindness all day, then pass them off to my sons in the evening."

"Mom, you and me both know you wouldn't let any child eat dessert before a meal, no matter how much you loved them."

She narrowed her eyes at him before cracking into a wide grin. "Alright, fair enough. But still, this house is awful empty. Surely it wouldn't be so bad if there were more people in here to fill it."

Before Sal could give his opinion one way or another, there was a knock at the side door. Neither of them had a chance to step towards it before Teddy opened it right up, a less bold Nova right behind her.

"Hey there, Mama Miller," Teddy said, quickly crossing the space to give the woman a peck on the cheek. "I just swung by to say hello. Gotta take a look at one of the combines. I'll be back around lunch!"

"I'll pen in some time for you," Mom called as the redhead practically zipped right out.

"Teddy caught me on my way to the front and had me follow her," Nova said sheepishly. "I hope that's alright."

"It's perfectly fine, don't you worry. The front door is so much farther anyway. Here, I've got another apron for you."

"What about my apron, Mom?" Sal teased gently only for her to throw one right at his face. Even in her elder years, his mother still had a great arm. "Thanks."

"Uh-huh, I know plenty of ladies like your looks, but don't think that means you can be cute with me," Mrs. Miller said.

"Yeah," Nova tacked on as she settled her own apron on. "Don't be *cute*, Sal."

But he was much more on his game than he was the previous day, and he shot her an impish look. "So you're saying you find me cute?"

"What? I—"

Mom cleared her throat, but the glare she sent him was more amused than anything reproachful. "Anyway, you ever made a good custard, Nova? They're tricky."

"Well, I accidentally end up scrambling them half the time. Don't know what's different between when I do them wrong or when I do them right, but there definitely is one."

Mom let out a huff. "I can't tell you how many custards I ruined that way in my early days. Here, come to the stove and I'll walk you through my foolproof way not to ruin them. Sal, if you could start measuring out for the recipes I have next to the bowls on the island, that would be perfect."

Sal did as she asked, but he kept one eye on them as he went about turning on the scales and reading over the directions. Maybe he should have been miffed at being relegated to what was essentially a child's task, but he didn't mind. He was just glad to be useful. How he felt in the kitchen with his mom and Nova was a whole lot different than how he felt sitting at his computer trying to finish up a budget proposal or a polish up a wooing email.

And if Mom and Nova weren't just the cutest pair. Both of them had looks of concentration on their face as the elder woman showed the younger what to do. It made Sal wonder what it would be like if he'd had a sister instead of all brothers. But of his father and two uncles, only one of them ended up having daughters, and that was the ranch out west. That was also the part of the family that didn't get along with McLintoc Miller at all, the final ties being cut after Simon's disastrous graduation party when insults had gone flying every which way.

Sal knew he'd seen the French girl and Mom make things together a couple of times, and Teddy would occasionally make picnic baskets for them to do their girls' date, or whatever it was they did, but he'd never seen anyone just take to baking like Nova was. That wasn't very fair. Maybe after the current wave was all said and done, Sal could make a concentrated effort to bake with Mom more often. Who cared what Dad said—if he even found out. It seemed like he hardly even left his study or boardrooms anymore.

Just like the day before, the hours started to slip away quickly between jokes, buzzing around the oven, and a seemingly endless list of things to do. But Sal liked it and almost wished it could go on forever, even if his lower back was starting to hurt from bending slightly over the island, and his eyes cross from reading the neatly typed out recipes his mom had laid out for him.

He didn't know how he never managed to get ahead, considering he had the easiest job, but he didn't mind that he never had to wait around for the next step. It seemed as soon as he had something fully measured out, either Nova or Mom would be there to take the bowl and combine it with whatever it was supposed to be added to and mixed however it was supposed to. Sal learned a lot, despite the whirring of several machines and the beeping of about a dozen different timers. Things like it was possible to beat the air out of eggs, and adding things in different orders at different temperatures could completely change a dessert's texture. And even that some things needed to be set in a pan full of water before being slid into the oven. Something about dispersing the temperature of the oven more evenly?

Whatever the reason, it was pretty clear that baking was some sort of chemical magic, and he had no idea how his mother had done so many of the baking splurges on her own before. No wonder she'd been up until the wee hours of the morning and snappish for the rest of the week. She'd been functionally performing her own culinary miracles and no one in the house so much as lent a hand—except, again, the aforementioned hired help.

Huh, they really had done wrong by her. Sal resolved to make that up to her in the future.

But for the moment, everything was all smiles. The custards came out great, apparently, and before Sal knew it, there was a knock on the side door and Teddy was strolling in.

"Oh gee, am I interrupting?" she asked, whistling at the sheer amount of baked goods all around them.

"Teddy!" Mom cried, looking at her watch. "It's one already? Where has the time gone?"

"Into your oven, apparently," the mechanic remarked with a grin. "Ooooh! Is that cheesecake?"

She reached out, but before she could so much as touch it, Mom was batting her hand away. "That needs to cool, young lady. You can have some when I take it to the community center tomorrow."

"No fair. You know I ain't never been much of one for patience."

"Well, you're going to have to learn. No cheesecake today."

Teddy made an over-the-top groan before winking at Nova, who chuckled lightly. "But on a more serious note, we can have lunch another day. I see you're busy here."

Mom looked like she was about to agree, but all of Sal's recent thoughts about his mom being lonely and needing more time to just have fun rushed him all at once. "Go with her," he blurted out, setting down his scoop once more.

"What was that, Sal?"

"I said go with her. Have a nice lunch. We can handle it in here for an hour or so. Right, Nova?"

"Oh yeah!" Nova answered with an enthusiastic nod. "All the custards are setting, the cheesecakes are cooling, you've pretty much only got sticky cinnamon buns and a couple more cookie batches left."

"Don't you mean biscuits?" Sal asked.

"Hey, don't get cute with me now."

It was a call back to the previous day's conversation, and it shouldn't have made him smile so hard, but it did. "So you still think I'm cute?"

Nova let out an exaggerated sigh, and Sal looked back to his mother. Naturally his peripheral vision caught Teddy giving him and Nova a *very* curious once over, but he chose to ignore that.

"See? We'll be fine. Go have fun."

"Well..." his mother seemed to waffle for another moment before clapping her hands. "You know what? I'm not going to argue. A blessing is a blessing, and although I love baking, it'll be nice to get off my feet for a while."

"Good to hear!" Teddy said, offering her arm. "I packed the

picnic basket, and it's already at our spot in the garden. I took some pictures of my black beauty peppers, by the way. They're really starting to blush towards their final color."

"Already! That's two weeks sooner than I expected!"

"Yeah, the anthocyanins in these ones are crazy!"

There were a few more sentences between the two that Sal knew were in English, but he didn't understand them, nonetheless. A few more moments later and the pair were gone entirely, leaving him and Nova in the kitchen.

Alone.

...sometimes he really needed to think his plans through better.

Nova spoke up first. "I'm going to grab a glass of water, and then how about after that we move onto the white chocolate chip and macadamia nut cookies?"

"Sounds good to me," Sal said, proud of how he sounded almost normal.

"You know, I was kinda surprised to see these on the list. Didn't know they were popular down here in Texas."

"They're not really, but they're Simon's favorite cookie, so I think Mom makes them out of habit."

"Simon? Which one is he? I don't remember... wait... he's the young one, right? At college or something?"

"Try or something. He announced at his graduation party that he was going backpacking around the world for six months." Sal paused for a moment, thinking. "Huh, in fact, that should be over real soon now. I wonder why he hasn't phoned in with plans to come home."

"Maybe he's not."

Now Sal stopped what he was doing for real, giving Nova his full attention. "What do you mean by that?"

"I mean, could be nothing, but when I first came to the

continental United States, I was just doing a summer abroad to connect with my American roots. Then I extended it until the holidays. Then it was a year abroad. And now I've just never left."

"You like the States that much?" he said, aiming for levity because the thought of losing another one of his brothers to somewhere else was too much. He *liked* Simon, even as flighty as the guy was.

"I like parts of the States. I love the rich blend of cultures. I love how small communities come together. The openness, the warmth. I know a lot of people complain about how loud or talkative Americans can be, but I love that I can go somewhere new and leave with three good conversations and one new friend. It's wonderful.

"But I'm not a fan of the obsession with money and the weird warping of what Jesus stood for."

"What do you mean by that?"

"Um... I'm not sure this is a discussion I should have with my boss. Ignore me."

He didn't like that, how she shut him out quickly. And he understood why. Technically sharing religion or politics wasn't always the best idea, but he wanted to know *more*.

"I'd like to hear it, please." He said it softer than he would have with anyone else. He didn't want her to feel pressured or manipulated. It was just that if he understood more of what made the woman tick, maybe he would be able to finally figure out why she always threw him for such a loop.

"Okay, um... it's just that the second most important commandment in the Bible is to love your neighbor as yourself, Jesus literally said that, but sometimes I see a whole lot of not loving when I turn on the TV. Sometimes I just have to turn it off for a while because the drama is too much."

"Come on," Sal said skeptically. "Most of the States isn't overly dramatic."

"Maybe," Nova said. "But it's hard to believe that when I see the stories of people harming each other with words and actions every single day. It's scary, and that's a part of the States I'm not overly fond of."

Sal felt himself getting defensive. He *loved* the States, and it was hard to hear someone say something negative about his home country. "Those are outlier cases."

"Are they?"

"I'm sure."

"But how do you know that?"

"Because I'm sure I would have seen at least one of these things happen if they were so common."

"You think so?" she asked.

Her tone was light, casual, but he could hear the determination under it. He wondered if he had really made a mistake in having her go on, but he was too caught up in the conversation to go back.

"Yeah."

"Okay, I can see how you might think that. But I'd like to propose an idea," Nova said.

"An idea?"

"Yeah. So, do you think that perhaps you, a multi-millionaire—"

"Billionaire."

"Right. Do you think that you, a billionaire who is presumably white and who lives on an estate forty-five minutes from the closest city, might have a very different life experience than say... a poor black girl from the inner city?"

Sal thought back to some of the insane stories he'd heard from Elizabeth, and then from Frenchie. Even a couple from

Teddy. The women's lives all seemed insane to him, even if he had been the one to figure out that the Frenchie girl was homeless in the park.

"I..."

Nova's voice was quieter when she continued. "You know, I was picked up by immigration once."

That stopped him cold right when he'd picked up his scoop again. "You what?"

"Got picked up. I was walking around with a couple of my friends, Yolanda and Daniella. Nice girls who I'd met when I'd first moved here and was confused in the supermarket. We were going out to the movies together when we all got picked up.

"It was one of the scariest experiences of my life. They hauled us away, took us to what seemed like a jail, and demanded our papers. We had our IDs, of course, but they kept saying that wasn't enough. They separated us, and I remember the officer who was talking to me kept accusing me of having a fake ID. Kept asking what my 'real' name was, not the white name I made up."

"They thought you weren't white?"

"That's what I'm guessing. I mean, I know I tan pretty deep, but I'm about as white bread as you can get. Irish, Welsh, and all that. I'm just what people seem to call 'ethnically ambiguous.' They held me there for hours before my immigration lawyer was able to call them and set them straight."

"I... I don't know what to say to that."

"That's alright. I just wanted you to know that we all have different life experiences. And while sometimes something seems impossible, listening to other folks might prove otherwise."

"What happened to your friends?"

"I don't know. I lost contact with them. For all that I'm aware, they were deported, or they packed up and moved. I've texted them, but nothing gets answered. We never did connect on social media so..." She shrugged, and Sal couldn't help but wonder about the life that the woman in front of him had lived.

"Why didn't you leave?" he asked.

"Hmmm?"

"That sounds so awful. I wouldn't blame you if you left the States altogether. But you didn't."

"No, I didn't."

She was closing off again. He could feel it. "... is there a reason?"

Finally, she stopped what she was doing, setting aside the spatula she had been stirring with. "I guess it's because even with all that awfulness, being in the States was a chance for me to be free. Appropriate, isn't it, considering that is the theme of the place and all that."

"Free?"

She nodded, and he could tell that she was picking her words carefully, one by one. It felt like something important was happening and his skin prickled with the weight of anticipation.

"Back home, who I am is already decided. I'm the too tall, too fat, too opinionated eldest daughter. I was basically used as a third parent to raise my siblings growing up, and nothing I did was ever good enough. I wasn't smart enough, wasn't pretty enough, wasn't *good* enough. I was a set of difficulties and failures, one right after the other.

"But here, I'm just Nova. A struggling twenty-one-year-old who fits right in with all the other struggling twenty-one-year-olds. I'm not anything special, or awful. I'm just *me*. And after nineteen years of trying to squeeze myself into being what my family wanted and utterly failing at that, it's a real nice feeling to just... *be*."

There was so much information in there, so much to unpack and digest. They'd gotten very serious, very quickly, but his brain was gobbling it up and hoarding every detail like a dragon.

Her family didn't like her? Seemed like insanity. Nova was tough—he'd watched her snap her own knee into place. Nova was kind—he'd seen her with animals, and how she acted with Mom was more than enough proof of that. She was capable—she wouldn't have gotten her job, otherwise. She was funny—the previous day had had Sal's cheeks hurting from how much he'd laughed and smiled. She was a litany of other positive traits, all of which surged on him at once. The idea that her parents could see her as anything other than a wonderful young woman was insane to him.

But he couldn't say any of that, because it was all too much. The air was thick with the entire weight of their exchange, which admittedly was a lot. They both needed a break, something to give them a moment to collect themselves.

Then it clicked. "Wait, you're only twenty-one?" he asked.

"Yeah. Why, how old did you think I was?"

"Well, considering how your body is already falling apart, I thought at least forty."

"Forty!" She gasped, mouth going wide. "Here I am, pouring my heart out to you, and you want to say you thought I was *forty*?"

There it was, the moment broke between them, all the talk of what was wrong with the States and her family was gone. Not forgotten, of course, her points had brought up several things that he had wanted to address later, but he put away for a reprieve.

"What's that? I couldn't hear you over the cracking of your crumbling knees."

"Why you!" she gestured with her spatula, threatening him via baking supplies, but what neither of them expected was for the whipped topping to fly from the thing and go sailing towards Sal, hitting him square in the chest.

"Oh, my gosh!" Nova said, rushing over, grabbing a dish-cloth on her way and dampening it in the corner sink. She walked over and stood in front of him, wiping at the center of his shirt. "I did *not* mean to do that! I'm so sorry!"

Sal tried not to think about how she was so close to him, and how his body was acutely aware of her every touch at the center of his chest. He could feel a blush rising to his cheeks like it was high school all over again. He needed another distraction.

Dragging his fingers through some of the flour on the kitchen island, he brought his hand up and flicked it right onto her own front, most of it hitting the apron but a small amount going above. Some even splashed up onto her chin, which frankly was impressive.

She stopped with her gentle dabbing and looked up at him.

"...did you just?"

But all he did was bat his eyes down at her. "Did I what?"

"Oh, cheeky, *cheeky*," she accused before her hand went right into the flour bag beside him and she slapped a whole handful to his front. The white powder went *everywhere*, and he knew he was going to be finding little bits of it in his hair for at least a week.

"I don't think you know what you're doing," he said, his

own hand hovering closer to the flour. But she just snatched it up and rushed around to the other side of the kitchen island, flicking more of the powder at him.

"Oh, I know exactly what I'm doing. Do you?"

"You're about to find out."

And that was how, at the ripe old age of twenty-six, Sal got into his first flour fight. It didn't last long, but it really didn't need to. He chased her around, Nova flicking flour at him with surprising accuracy until he was able to get into his mother's secondary supply. Then it was more even, with the two of them ducking behind the counters and island respectively, making quite the mess of things and completely wasting supplies.

But it was *fun*. It was fun and both of them were laughing, and Sal felt like he could float right out of all of his troubles for at least a little while. It was just so silly. When was the last time he had been allowed to be silly with no repercussions? No lectures about decorum or needing to represent his family?

He didn't know, and that complete lack of an answer made him enjoy himself that much harder.

And who knew how long the war would have kept on if a timer didn't go off, startling Nova to let out one of her classic yelps. Looking around, she realized that one of the mixers was still going and rushed over to turn it off.

"I think I got it in time," she said, breathing in relief as she sagged against the counter.

"It's just a mixer; it's not like it's going to burn anything."

"Yeah, but it is possible to over-beat something and completely ruin it. We just got the stiff peaks we wanted, so if we let it keep going, it would probably just break down entirely."

Sal shook his head, a soft rain of flour coming down onto

his shoulders. "Still don't know how you and Mom know all this baking stuff."

"Ha! She knows a lot more than me. But one thing I do know is we better clean this place up before your mum gets back."

Sal blinked then looked around at the kitchen. While it certainly wasn't the *worst* that it had ever been, there certainly was a *lot* of flour on the floors and over the one counter that Nova had been hiding behind.

"Yeah, that sounds like a good idea."

17

Nova

*N*ova flexed her hand, letting go of her death grip on the icing bag.

"You okay there?" Sal asked from right beside her. She could practically feel the gravitational pull of his body next to her. It was probably just in her mind, but he was just so *big*, so imposing, that it was impossible to ignore. "I think your knuckles have turned paper white."

"Yeah, yeah. Just concentrating."

"Oh, is that all? Looks like you're taking out some frustration on that poor icing bag."

"Everything's fine." Nova gave a nervous chuckle. "I'll work harder on having the appropriate facial expression for baking."

"I'm not sure there is a correct expression, but I'll believe you."

"Yeah, you better. All you're doing is mixing the icing. I'm the one piping it into bags and decorating the cookies."

"You know, I'm pretty sure Mom doesn't need these to be super fancy."

"I know, she wrote just to cover the cupcakes with a little rosette, but I... I kinda..."

"Want to impress her?" Sal supplied helpfully.

"Yeah. Is that silly? It probably is, isn't it?"

"Nah. I always want to impress my mom. She has that way about her."

"She's real nice, you know?"

"Oh yeah, I know. I am keenly aware."

Nova smiled to herself. Despite the persistent pain in her hand, she was having such a lovely time. Who would have known that she would find such comfort in the kitchen of a billionaire family?

"It's different. It's not something I'm used to."

"Yeah, judging by what you've told me of your family, that's understandable."

Nova let out a hum of agreement, flexing her hand again and then going back to icing. She'd done the rosettes, but now she was adding delicate little filigree.

"You want to try one?" she asked when she finished the cupcake and set it to the side with all the others.

"Sure, I bet they're tasty."

She batted his giant hand away from the dozen or so desserts she'd finished. "I meant do you want to try *icing* one."

But Sal just affixed her with a teasing look. "Given that one of my fingers is almost the same size as your wrist, what do you think the more reasonable interpretation of that is?"

"Your fingers are not the size of my wrist!" she objected, although her own laugh interrupted her. Since when was Sal so *funny*? If she'd known he was witty, maybe she wouldn't have been so brusque to him in the horse stables.

...then again, he *had* been acting awful weird at the time.

"Close enough."

"Pfft, I think not. I'm a solid woman."

"Is that what you are?"

She felt another chuckle rise up through her. Goodness, her abs were sore from all the laughing and mirth she'd let loose in the past couple of days. "It's not my entire definition, but it's definitely at least an important footnote."

"What would be your entire definition then?"

Nova set down her piping bag again, letting out a long breath. Her eyes swung to Sal and she was surprised by how intense his green eyes were as they stared at her. That same look had intimidated her before, made her feel awkward. Off-center. But after a day and a half stuck in a small kitchen, that same look... kinda thrilled her.

Her heart rate was picking up and her tongue came out to wet her suddenly dry lips. She didn't miss how Sal's gaze followed the movement of her tongue, and if that just didn't make her face heat up like a fire was on it.

"That's a loaded question if I ever heard one, my friend."

"Is that what our definition is then?"

She blinked at him, thrown. "What?"

"Is that what we are? Friends?"

Oh boy. It was not fair for him to sound like *that*, while looking at her like *that*, with a face like *that*. She remembered reading once that God never let someone face a temptation that was stronger than they could bear, but *goodness* he was playing dirty when he handcrafted Salvatore Miller.

"I'd like to think so, if that's not too informal," she managed to say.

Was the oven door open? Because suddenly her palms were sweaty and the air seemed thick. Maybe the air conditioning needed to be cranked up? That certainly couldn't hurt anything, and maybe it would make her feel more grounded.

Because at the moment, she felt like she was floating away from sanity, swept up in the moment and the warmth in her heart, and in the undeniable pull of Sal.

She'd gotten angry at him before—when he'd been shirtless and obviously trying to make her flustered. But anger wasn't anywhere on her docket in the kitchen, if only because it seemed like he was genuinely interested in their conversation. Not trying to manipulate her or embarrass her.

It just turned out that his genuine interest made her feel kind of like a high school girl in the presence of a *very* hot college frat boy. Out of her league and probably inappropriate.

"I don't think that's too informal, no. As long as you don't tackle me again."

"Promise me you won't go about killing innocent animals or reptiles, and you have a deal."

"Unless they're in the house, I'll keep my hands to myself."

"Alright then, deal."

She offered her hand to him and he took it, his large fingers engulfing hers. It was a bit over-the-top and maybe a lot silly, but they gave one hearty shake before breaking out in laughter again.

"Why do I feel like I just sold my soul or something?" Sal said.

"Not your soul," she corrected, feeling giddy. "Just your friendship. Which, you know, is almost as important."

"Ah, I see. Well, I guess I'm just gonna have to trust you, then."

"Worse choices have been made," Nova shot right back

before returning to her piping. Her hand was *screaming* at her, but it would be worth it to see Mum Miller's face.

That was one of Nova's biggest flaws, she supposed. She loved pleasing people, craved seeing that happy look on their faces. But with everything she'd gone through with her family, she rarely trusted anyone enough to allow herself to care.

But she trusted Mum Miller. Or at least she was pretty sure that she did. The woman made her feel welcome, something Nova had forgotten she was even missing. If someone was an outsider their whole life, it was easy to get used to such a thing.

A companionable silence settled onto them again as she continued to ice. Eventually, however, she realized that Sal was done with his mixing and just waiting next to her, quiet and still. And yet she was more than comfortable beside him, like they'd been friends forever already. Which was pretty ridiculous considering that she'd just been complaining about him in physical therapy to a random old woman a week or so earlier.

Funny how things could flip like that.

"So, since we're friends, can I ask you a question?" she said cautiously after she finished another cupcake, setting the piping bag down for the third time and rotating her wrist experimentally.

"That sounds very weighted, just so you know."

"Probs 'cause it is, mate."

The corner of Sal's mouth quirked at that. "Fair enough. I'll bite."

"What's going on with your family?"

He stiffened at that, his face going carefully blank. "What do you mean?"

"Oh, don't you 'what do you mean' me, you know what I'm

talking about. The tension with you and your brothers, the shouting with your dad. Everything. It's permeating this whole place."

"It's that obvious, huh?"

"You Millers are not exactly subtle. By any definition of the word."

He huffed a laugh at that, but it was dry. Laced with bitterness that came from somewhere deep inside of him. Ow, Nova could feel that sharp, biting snappiness inside of her own chest.

"I guess you can say that right now, we're having a difference of opinion."

"Aw, come on now, don't give me a politician's answer. Lay it on me straight."

He didn't respond at first, his careful expression shifting into a frown that was growing deeper by the second. Oh. Maybe she *shouldn't* have asked him about his family.

But eventually he began to speak again, his words stilted and as awkward as before. Huh, that was an interesting development.

"My father is our patriarch, I guess. A pretty conservative guy. And he's built his empire a certain way that's been incredibly successful. My brothers and I owe our whole lives, all the luxury to him. But now my brothers are sort of, banding together, and trying to change everything."

"Change everything how?"

"Oh, you know how."

"No actually, I don't. Believe it or not, I'm not exactly in on the comings and goings of your family."

"Ah... right." His eyes flicked away from her, that intense look in them long gone. It was the uncertain Sal in front of her again, and it was telling to see what made him uncomfortable, what made him falter, and what didn't.

"You know, bleedin' heart stuff."

"Bleeding... heart...stuff?" He nodded as if that was enough. "I'm sorry, Sal, but you're going to have to give me more to go on. If that's an American expression, I don't think I know it."

Sal let out a frustrated sound, his gaze flicking back to her, but just barely. "You know, blathering on about a living wage that's *well* over the industry standard, more insurance benefits. Vacation time. And all the animal stuff too."

"The animal stuff?"

"Yeah. You don't want to know how much we've spent in the past year because of Sterling's girlfriend. It's in the million-dollar range, and they're still going."

"Sal, your family's whole livelihood depends on animals."

"Yeah, but that doesn't mean we need to make them five-star resorts. We treat them well enough."

...there was so much there to work through, but Nova kept her mouth shut. She wanted Sal to trust her with opening up, so she needed to let him finish. "I see."

"And then there's all this talk about needing to expand welfare programs, helping the poor, and their weird attitude towards the church my family sponsored."

"The same church that your mum is making food for?"

"Yeah, that's the food pantry that Solomon took over. He and the others are obsessed with these handout programs, but these people aren't going to learn anything if you just *hand* stuff to them."

That was a red flag if she had ever heard one. "These people?"

"Yeah, the poor and all that. The French girl's type. Did you know she was homeless and living in the park when my brother met her? And he only met her because she was defacing the church!"

"Defacing it how?"

"Spray painting it."

"*Oh*, was she the one I read about in the news? Who was tagging places with political messages?"

Sal nodded. "That was how Solomon ended up finding her again."

What a small world. "Really? That's insane. I loved her stuff."

"You..." he sputtered a moment, as if the very idea was unfathomable to him. "You loved her stuff?"

"Yeah. Thought most of it was pretty apropos. Did you stop and think about what they meant?"

"What do you mean, 'what they meant'? It's *graffiti*."

"You think graffiti can't be art?"

"Well, most art I know of isn't painted illegally on the side of buildings."

"Then I'd say you've got a pretty narrow understanding of art. Just look at how popular Banksy is."

"Who?"

She sighed. "I'll explain later. Point being, I get it. Your brothers and your father have some very different ideals all of a sudden, and you're sort of in the middle."

"I'm not in the middle," Sal stated so sharply that it almost startled her. "I'm with my dad, who founded this ranch and built it from the ground up. He's a self-made man!"

"Oh," Nova said, as emotionless as she could.

"Oh?"

"Yeah, oh."

"That wasn't just an 'oh.' That had a tone."

"Did it?" she asked.

He gave her a look that she was pretty sure he learned right from his mum.

She continued, "Your father is a self-made man?"

"Yup, as real as they come."

Nova continued to try keeping her voice even-toned. "How'd he get the money to start the ranch? Nobody just makes a mega ranch in one generation without significant resources."

"Oh, he had his own trust set up by his father. Got it when he was twenty-one. With that and some investors, he was ready to go."

"Right. And how much did his father give him?"

"I mean, I don't know that. But I imagine at least several million. You know, seed money," Sal said.

"Right, so he's a self-made man, but he was given more money than someone might normally see in their entire lifetime."

"I..."

Nova knew she had to be careful what she said next. "Look, I don't feel the need to convert you or anything like that, but you seem pretty unhappy with things, so I just wonder..."

"What?"

"Have you ever stopped and thought about what if your brothers were right?" she said. He opened his mouth far too quickly and Nova pointed her piping bag at his face. "Nuh-uh. I'm not saying they *are* right, but I'm asking if you've stopped—really stopped—and thought about the things they're saying rather than dismissing them right from the get-go?"

He didn't answer for a moment, chewing his lip before sighing. And it was like his stiff posture melted all at once, his chin resting in his palm as he leaned against the island. "No. I haven't."

"Your brothers seem to be pretty smart guys. And I know Elizabeth and Teddy are smart. I haven't spent much time with that French lady you mentioned, but I'm sure she's gotta be sharp if Solomon is into her.

"So if you know all these people are smart, wouldn't it be worth it to try to understand why they think the way they think?"

"I... I suppose."

He was uncomfortable, she could tell that, but she pressed on. She found herself leaning towards him as she did, caught up in her own earnestness.

To be honest, she disagreed with a lot of what he'd said, and from anyone else she would have shut down the conversation and stopped talking to them entirely. But with Sal it felt like the words weren't his own, but rather he was parroting something that he had heard so many times that he had never stopped to question it.

"I've heard about this community center a couple of times, and it's clear your mum is pretty jazzed about it. It seems like it's helping a lot of people. The kind of people who don't get millions of dollars of seed money from their parents."

"It is. They have afterschool programs for the kids and all that."

"And do you think the kids are wrong to use those? Should they be able to pull themselves up by their own bootstraps?"

He looked at her like she was crazy, and that was enough to give her hope. "What? No. If anything, the kids are the innocent ones in this, paying for the poor decisions of their parents."

Okay, maybe he was about halfway to the point, but that was better than nothing.

"I'm glad the kids are being helped," he said. "I'd never object to that."

"Gotcha." It was a small victory, them being able to see eye to eye. Part of her knew that she should leave it there, but another part of her wanted to keep going.

She was greedy, she supposed. Her dad had always said that enough was never enough for her. That she always had to push for more. Always had to be right. But her mouth was still moving, and words were coming out of it, so maybe they weren't so wrong.

"So don't you think that maybe, with the kids being helped, the poor being helped, and the workers being helped, that it might be worth a tiny loss of profit? It's not like your family is hurting at all."

"It's not as simple as that."

"Isn't it? Money is just money. It's not *real*. Not like human life. Not like happiness or love or any of those other things that truly bring us together." She knew she was getting preachy, but she was all caught up in her own point.

He was staring at her again, an unreadable expression on his face.

"Is that really how you see the world?"

"Of course. Like, for example, how I feel about animals. I love helping them. I love making sure they're safe and warm and assured. And I feel that way about my fellow man too. There's more to life than just profit. There's the comfort we get from sharing a smile. The security of knowing that your neighbors have food and shelter and you do too.

"I want everyone I know to be protected, to be safe. And sure, there are some things we can't defend from like tornados or wildfires or those who seek to hurt others, but there are others that we can. Or at least we should.

"As long as I have food, I'll never let any friend or acquaintance of mine go hungry." Her voice was rising, and she could feel her cheeks flushing as she grew more passionate, but she couldn't stop. She was caught up in the ideal world inside her head, one where everyone was fed and safe and didn't have to worry about bills or being one missed paycheck away from their world crumbling. "If I have water, no one I know will go thirsty. If I had enough of your mum's baked goods, I'd want to share them with the whole city until every person knew how good they were.

"If I could stop every snake or lizard from being panic-slaughtered, if I could save every dog or cat that was being neglected, if I could stop every racehorse from being abused, I would in a second. Even if that means I'd never have a chance at having billions, or even millions."

There was that intense gaze again, like he was seeing down to her core. He had turned completely towards her, his head dipped down so that they were closer than they had ever been.

Excitement raced through her. Nova felt like she was getting to him, *really* getting to him. Poor Sal, how long had he been alone? Caught between what his brothers had learned and what his father stubbornly clung to? What was it Aunt Kini had told her? That she could be a shining light for him? A sort of guide? In that moment, she found the desire to be just that bubbling up in her, hot and bright and ready to lead.

"You'd do all that?"

"And so much more, Sal. I think it's crazy that you don't realize how much you could change everything if you wanted to."

He blinked at that, and she had a momentary reprieve from his stare. "Me?"

"Yeah. If I had a million dollars, just one, oh *man*. I would start an after-school program too. Maybe something about urban gardening to give people more food security. Definitely things like sewing, baking, cooking, and basic car maintenance. I would pay off the medical debt of everyone in the building. Probably every one of my friends.

"Maybe I'd pay everyone's rent for a month too, just to do it. I'd go out to eat and I'd tip the waitress five hundred, maybe even a thousand dollars just to see her face. I'd buy my friends all the things that they'd been needing but couldn't because money was too tight. I'd make sure they all got to the dentist too.

"I'd invest in something, I don't know what, but something with interest and then I would use that interest to make a scholarship. Maybe for college, or maybe just for one of those fancy high schools that look good on college applications. And that's just with a single million.

"You have so much more than that, Sal. Doesn't that make you want to do something like your brothers are? You're so smart, and you have so *much*, you could completely change the course of hundreds and hundreds of people's—"

She had more to say, because of course she did, but suddenly Sal's large hands wrapped around either side of her waist and he pulled her to him, nearly toppling her out of her chair. Her first instinct was to object, but the words weren't coming out of her mouth. Her entire brain froze for a moment, confused because she had been so certain that she was just hitting her stride with her impromptu sermon, but when it finally rebooted, she realized she couldn't say anything because Sal was *kissing* her.

She was surprised. No, *shocked*, her mind flatlining again at the impossibility of it all. Salvatore Miller was kissing her! And for the slightest of breaths, it felt so *nice*. His hands were so warm and solid against her side, holding her securely, safely. The scent of him was in her nose, all masculinity and cleanliness, with something like sandalwood just underneath. Her heart thundered at the feel of his mouth against hers, lips pressed against each other, his desire so apparent in the way they demanded a response from her.

But once that breath was over, she realized exactly what was happening, and it was as if ice was dumped down her soul.

He was her *boss*. That was way wrong. She'd be silly to think a relationship with Sal could go anywhere, do anything but hurt her. And he hadn't even asked to kiss her. He'd just taken it. He was older than her. Stronger than her. He could do anything he wanted, and what could she do about it? Fight back, sure, but it wasn't a fight she could win. Nova hadn't been born yesterday. She knew how it worked with rich folks getting their way.

Her hands came up to his chest and she *shoved* with all that she had. That was enough, apparently, because Sal's tall chair tipped back, and he let go of her.

He looked confused, bewildered even, and if that didn't make just about zero sense. She sputtered something, words trying to come back to her, but she felt like she had been launched into an entirely different universe.

"*What?*" Sal asked with a curious expression on his face. Like he hadn't just grabbed her and kissed her senseless without permission right in the middle of his mother's kitchen.

For the first time in her life, Nova was truly at a loss for words. Instinct taking over, her hand whipped out and the next thing she knew, a deafening crack filled the room as her palm connected with Sal's cheek.

"Keep your hands off me," she managed to say, her lungs feeling like they were little more than wet tissue paper. She didn't wait around to see what he said, instead hightailing it out of there before he could stop her.

And she didn't stop running until she reached her car. She knew better than to do so much as pause. She had to get home to where she was safe.

But considering how easily Sal could access her records, the only safe part about her apartment and its flimsy door was that it was hopefully just far enough away to be inconvenient to him.

Oh boy, she really messed up.

18

Salvatore

*S*al stared into the mirror, looking at his cheek.

There was no sign that he had even been struck hours earlier, and yet he felt it nonetheless. The hot, burning outline of Nova's hand as she'd slapped him with what hadn't exactly been a modest amount of force.

But it was really the look on her face that seemed to stab right through his chest. She'd looked so *scared*. Terrified even. Scared and full of anger and so unhappy.

Had his kiss really been so awful? It wasn't like he had planned it, but he'd been so caught up in the moment. Nova's bright cheeks and the way her eyes sparkled as she talked about everything she'd do if only she had a million dollars. Her voice was full of hope and warmth, and he believed every word she said. She was just so *kind* to him, and she seemed to make Mom happy without even trying. He'd seen her sing and joke to animals when she didn't think anyone was watching.

If he could have just an ounce of that goodness, maybe he could be more like her. Maybe his brothers or his dad would like him more. Maybe he'd feel less empty.

And so he'd kissed her. He'd kissed her because he'd wanted her, wanted to be more like her, wanted to know what it was like to have someone so pretty and *good* as her in his arms.

...wanted to know what if felt like for someone like *her* to want someone like *him*.

Now he just wanted to throw up.

He'd messed up; he'd *really* messed up, but his pride was snarling at the thought. There were dozens, maybe even hundreds of women who would give anything to be in the same position that Nova had been in, and she'd struck him. Just slapped him out of nowhere.

...but those hundreds of women weren't Nova. They didn't know him like she did, didn't fearlessly call him out when they disagreed with him. Nova tackled him outright when she thought he was going to hurt something innocent.

And the worst part?

That kiss had been something else. Unlike anything else he'd ever felt. Her lips were so soft, heated against his, and that floral scent of hers made him crazy.

But then he'd remembered how she looked so frightened and his vivid, amorous fantasy vanished in a puff of smoke.

He'd scared her, and he was only just beginning to kind of get why. Like with every few minutes that passed, he could see more of how it came across to her.

They hadn't been doing anything particularly romantic. He hadn't asked her. He had six inches on her and probably around a hundred pounds. She was strong, sure, he knew that from her tackling him, but his biceps were almost the size of her head.

She'd been alone in his home, off-center, and had practically fallen off her chair. To him it had been all passion and revelation as he was caught up in her personal magnetism. Because she was so incredible, so passionate and open and kind.

But to her... yeah, the thought of how it might have been from her perspective made him shudder. He was basically her boss, and he'd come onto her without asking. Just assuming she was feeling what he was. When obviously, she hadn't been at all.

Yeah, he had *definitely* messed up.

He turned off the light in the bathroom so he wouldn't have to look at his own face anymore. Standing there in the dark, he tried to see a way out of his own mess. But every time he recalled Nova's face and her expression—which were all too easy to picture in the pitch-black—he felt sick to his stomach. It was getting worse and worse as more time passed.

His stomach churned, and he realized he was out of his depth. His body went through the motions as he dried off, put on evening loungewear, and left his room. Eventually, he found himself in the twins' wing. Theirs was actually the smallest out of the whole family, after having switched with Simon in his senior year of high school.

It wasn't hard to find them in their gym, laying out on the mats and bouncing a ball off the ceiling back and forth to each other. They weren't even talking, just communicating in that silent way of theirs. For a moment, Sal allowed himself to be jealous of their closeness. All of the brothers had drifted with age, that much was obvious, but the twins had always had each other. Two sides of the same coin, at least they would never truly be alone.

"Hey," he said as he opened the door. Silas tipped his head back to look at him while Sterling sat all the way up. They clearly hadn't been expecting him, but Sal hadn't exactly planned his trek out either.

"Hey, Sal, what's up?"

For just a breath, he entertained the idea of turning around and leaving them mystified. He hated admitting his mistake in front of people, if only because they were usually used against him later. But what choice did he have? He needed help.

"I've done something wrong and I don't know how to fix it. Or if it can even be fixed."

The two exchanged a look, doing that twin-talk thing again, before Sterling gestured his hand for Sal to take a seat beside them. "We're happy to listen. Come have a seat."

Sal took the offer, settling next to them. It was almost like back in high school, when he would come to them with girl problems or needing help with homework. How long had it been since he'd trusted them enough to be vulnerable in front of them?

It felt like a whole age. He was uncomfortable and his pride was outright *spitting*, but he put that all aside and began to explain.

19

Nova

*N*ova was going to lose her job.

She was sure of it, so sure of it that she had been pacing her apartment for hours, working herself into a tizzy, and wondering if she should start to apply for jobs. Or maybe she should apply for unemployment and skip town so she didn't have to worry about repercussions for striking a billionaire for the second time.

She was screwed. She was *so* monumentally screwed.

Her mother always said she didn't think—that she was so sure of what was right and wrong that she didn't stop and think about what was *best*. And nowhere on the best list was slapping her employer across the face.

But she also knew that it wasn't wrong of her to defend herself. That he had no right to kiss her. That had been rude, it had been invasive, and it made her feel... *weak*.

Nova hated feeling weak.

Yet, at the same time, she was struggling internally. She was *very* attracted to Sal. From his thick hair to his blazing green eyes, to his stubborn chin and to that ridiculously jacked body of his. But it was more than just his looks. He was funny. He was clearly a mama's boy in a cute way, not a creepy way. He was lost, like her, just wanted to be accepted and loved, like her. He was gentle and patient and a great listener.

He also had a *lot* of issues to work through. Big ol' red flag issues.

And it was arrogant to think she could be some sort of leader for him. She couldn't be a "guiding light" and also an employee of his family and *also* mack on him like a lovesick high schooler. Not to mention that he was older than her, richer than her, and *bigger* than her.

Nova was a smart girl. She knew that all of those things were risks. Sure, not all men were predators. Heck, she'd even go out on a limb and say that most of them weren't. But the trouble was there was no way to know who was who until she was put into a vulnerable situation, and well, if Sal hadn't just put her right into one.

Thank goodness it was Friday, at least. She spent the weekend hiding in her home, sure at any time her phone would ring, or a knock would sound at her door and that would be that. She would be happy if she was just fired. Anxieties and terrors about him showing up at her home, or sending a threatening letter played through her head too.

...but at the same time, she didn't want to believe that Sal would do that. She didn't want to think that she'd been that duped about his character. Sure, maybe he turned out to be a playboy and had made way too forward of a pass at her, but that didn't mean he was evil.

Or at least, that was what she hoped. She supposed she had no way of knowing.

And that might have been the actual worst part.

When Monday rolled around, she'd called and taken the day off. When Elizabeth didn't ask why and there weren't any angry calls or emails, she almost began to wonder if maybe, just maybe, she might be able to keep her job despite what she'd done. She didn't get an answer, of course, but on Tuesday she decided to go in.

Sal was nowhere to be found, and no one treated her any differently. Despite that, she still jumped at every sound, so sure that the hammer was going to drop at any second. But there was no slamming of hammers or the other shoes, or anything, and she went home that night without incident.

Wednesday passed. Thursday. Nova began to breathe again, feeling assured that Sal was too prideful to tell anyone what she had done and wasn't some vengeful movie villain. But all of that certainty vanished when she saw him waiting by her car as she went to head home for another weekend.

Nova froze, dropping her keys to the ground. Her mind shot in a million different directions, trying to think if anyone was close enough and the quickest way to escape. Sal was faster than her, despite his bulk, and her knee was iffy to begin with. Maybe she could—

He held up his hands, taking a step back, and that cut off her frantic escape plans.

"I'm not here to start anything," he said, sounding miserable. And that in and of itself was enough to keep her mind from spinning wildly into a panic. He wasn't moving to attack. That was good.

"What do you want?" she asked, proud of the steel in her voice. He didn't need to know how afraid she was. Or how torn. Because at the moment, he looked so utterly upset and ashamed that it actually made her heart twist. How bizarre was that?!

"I just want to apologize."

Apologize? "...okay."

"Okay?"

"Okay," she repeated. "But make it quick. And don't come any closer."

He nodded, slowly lowering his hands. "Okay, yeah. I can do that." He took a deep breath, and it seemed like with a great deal of effort, he was able to raise his gaze to meet her own. "Look, I am real, *real* sorry about what happened in the kitchen. I didn't mean to scare you, please believe that, but I completely understand why I did. I crossed a professional boundary, which I never should have, and I took something from you without permission."

...whoa. That was an actual apology. She would be lying if she didn't admit that she had been expecting some half-spun thing about her over-reacting or how she led him on. It wasn't the first time a guy had come onto her in her life, and she doubted that it would be the last. But Sal didn't seem to be done in the slightest, each of his words surprising her more than the previous one.

"I broke the trust that you gave me and abused my position over you as one of your employers. I realize that, and that I was wrong, and I just want you to know that I am deeply, deeply sorry for my actions. I'm not asking your forgiveness, because I know that's not something I'm owed, but I wanted to clarify that there's not going to be any repercussions for you standing up for yourself." His expression grew even more miserable.

"I know how the world works. And I can't blame you for thinking what you did. I'll never really know what it's like to be in the position I put you in. But your job is safe here, and I'll never bother you again. I didn't kiss you out of some sort of malice, or because I felt you owed it to me. I was just... I just..." He sighed and looked down at his feet. "I messed up, is all. I'm sorry."

Nova stood there, completely stunned by the whole thing. That was about the best apology she'd ever been handed, and it was about the last thing she'd ever expected.

"I—"

"You don't have to say anything," Sal murmured. "Just wanted to make sure you knew you were safe. Your job is safe."

She nodded slowly. She knew that that should be the end of the conversation, that she should just walk away and leave well enough alone. But the relief that was flooding her combined with the achiness in her chest from just how *upset* Sal looked had her mouth moving.

Because he didn't look sad that he had to apologize, if that was possible. He looked pained like he was recalling what he had done and was ashamed of his actions. People messed up all the time, misinterpreted things, did dumb stuff, but Nova couldn't remember once someone just admitting to it and telling her that she was right. She wasn't being overdramatic. She wasn't too self-righteous. Sal understood why she did what she did and didn't try to justify his actions, even one ounce.

What was she supposed to say to that? She was prepared for a fight, or intimidation, or to have to defend why she dared to slap him... but none of that was happening. None of it.

"Mom doesn't know what happened. I told her that you'd gotten a bad headache and went home. I'll tell her, if you want me to, that I crossed a line.

"Look, I know I have no right to, but Mom was really

looking forward to asking you to hand out some of the baked goods this weekend. I won't go anywhere near it. I'll get Silas or Sterling to do it, but it would mean the world to her if you would still want to, you know, hang out with her."

Nova may not have known either of them long, but it was clear to see how much Sal enjoyed spending time with his mother. If he was giving up an important event just to make sure she was comfortable... well... that had to mean something, right?

"I'm willing to forgive you," she said in a rush, making her own cheeks burn. She was probably doing the wrong thing. She was probably being rash. But something in her heart told her to give him a second chance. That maybe, just maybe, if she gave him an inch to grow that he would truly flourish. "*If* you swear to never do that again. Don't *ever* put your hands on me without permission outside of some sort of emergency. No picking me up, no hands on my waist and no..." Her voice cracked ever so slightly, but she pushed past it. "...*kissing*."

"Right. Absolutely. I promise. And I'm sorry again. I never meant to be rude. I just... wasn't thinking. And thank you. Mom will be real happy. Silas is usually more—"

"You can come."

"What?" He seemed just about as shocked by that as she was that she said it.

But she swallowed and kept going.

"I accept your apology and believe it, so I'm giving you a chance to prove you're sincere." She felt her tone soften, a strange feeling bubbling in her chest. "I liked hanging out with you, Sal. You're fun. You're *funny*. But you scared me real bad. I didn't know what was happening or if it was going to escalate, and you have a whole lot of power over me and could ruin my life."

"I didn't think—"

"Yeah, I know you didn't. And maybe that's why I'm willing to sweep this under the rug. I want things to go back to how they were, Sal. It just might take some time."

"Thanks," he answered, voice strained. "That... that means a lot."

She gave him a nod and that seemed to be the end of it. He tipped his head politely and walked off, head ducked down like he really was ashamed of himself and embarrassed by what had happened.

Nova watched him go, hoping against hope that he would stick to his word, because her heart felt like he would. But in the back of her mind, she couldn't help but hear her mother's voice questioning her, asking her if she had really done the right thing.

What a bother.

20

Nova

"Can I pwease haf a sugar cookie with the pink frostin'?"

Nova bent forward, leaning over the wide table to see a little tyke who didn't quite make it over the top enough to see without standing on his tiptoes.

"Oh, hello there. You said you wanted one with pink frosting?"

He nodded. "It's my mama's favorite color. I wanna surprise her."

"Is that so? What about you? Don't you want anything?"

He looked out at the spread before him. It wasn't quite as massive as the mega-bake that Nova had helped with, but apparently those had all been delivered and gobbled up by the folks they were meant to go to. What they had laid out wasn't meager by any means, but it did make Nova wonder just how *much* Mum Miller baked every week. When she had asked the matriarch, she'd demurely said she did what she could when the weather was warm and that was that.

"Um... I dunno. I, uh..."

"Can you not see all that's up here?"

He shook his head, his cheeks turning bright pink in that way that only a little kid's could. Gosh, he was adorable. Maybe Mum Miller's desire for grandbabies was understandable.

"Here, lemme help," she said, rounding the table. "May I pick you up?"

"You sure? Mama says I'm gettin' heavy."

"Don't worry about it. I'm very strong."

"...okay. I wanna see."

He was a solidly built little kid, one that you could tell was going to shoot up as a teen and probably eat his sweet mama out of house and home. But solid or not, Nova wrapped an arm around him and hauled him up to look over the wares.

"*Wow*, there's a whole lot."

"Yeah, Mrs. Miller loves to bake, doesn't she?" Nova said, a smile finding its way on her face from both the boy's wonder and just thinking about all the fun she'd had in Mum Miller's kitchen. Sure, there had been a massive train wreck right at the end, but it had been mostly good.

"There's gotta be like, uh, at least twenty hundred here."

Nova looked over the nearly hundred different small baggies or containers they had laid out neatly across the flat surface of the table. "Wow! How'd you know there was that many here?"

"Wassat?" he rolled right along, one of his arms pointing to a white, fluffy slice in a plastic shell. Nova shifted him to her hip so she could carry him with one arm then reached for it.

"This is angel food cake."

He gasped like that truly was a revelation. "Did real angels make it?"

Nova couldn't help it as her gaze slid to Mum Miller, who had wandered away from the tables to help a gaggle of very young girls draw out a hopscotch ladder on the ground. Nova couldn't hear them from where she was, but they were all laughing and smiling and looking like they were just having a grand ol' time. "You know what, I think they might have."

"Okay, I wan' the angel food very much pwease, ma'am."

"Good choice!" Nova set him down and handed him both the cookie and the slice of cake. "I hope you enjoy it. Remember to have lots of fun and always be nice to everybody."

"Okay." He started to walk away, but something stopped him at the last moment, and he turned back to her. "Why d'you sound so funny? Are *you* an angel?"

Out of the mouths of babes. "Am I a what now?"

"My *tia* said that angels speak their own language."

"Oh well, that may be true, but I'm not an angel. I'm a regular human, I'm just from someplace very far away. Have you ever heard of Great Britain?"

The boy nodded very solemnly, like they truly were discussing something of biblical proportions. "There's a queen there, I think."

"Yes! That's very good. There's a queen there and a whole royal family and a lot of other fun stuff."

"And y'all sound diff'int?"

"Yes, we all sound different. Just like northerners up here sound different from the people you know."

"Oh, okay. Woulda been cooler if you were an angel."

"You know what, I don't think I can disagree on that. Angels are pretty cool."

"Well, that's okay. I like you anyway. Thank you, ma'am."

"No problem little guy. I hope to see you around."

"Okie dokies, artichokies!"

He turned to skip away, heading towards a woman who had three other children all demanding her attention. That must be "Mama." She looked nice enough, a smile around her face as she tried to pay attention to each of the little ones around her in turn. Nova felt the slightest little trickle of jealousy run through her, but she quickly dismissed it. The past was in the past, and that's where it would stay.

She turned to go back to the spot she was supposed to be in behind the table only to nearly jump out of her skin when she realized she wasn't alone. Frenchie was standing there, her arms crossed and her eyes right on Nova.

"What's up?" Nova asked in what she hoped was a friendly manner and not startled. For being such a tiny little thing, it was intimidating to be stared down by the artist. Of all the partners on the ranch, she was the one that Nova knew the least about.

"You were real good with that kid."

Oh, a compliment. Nova let her shoulders relax and shrugged. "He was cute, and he wanted something to treat his mum. Certainly better behaved than I probably was at his age."

She nodded, chewing at her lip, and Nova felt like something important was going on in the young woman's mind.

"I've got a few jumpy ones that are nervous about coming 'round here. Think if I bring 'em to you that you can work your charm on them? Make 'em comfortable?"

Nova blinked at her. "Why are they nervous?"

But she just waved her hand. "Think you can do it, or not?"

"Uh, sure. I'll do my best."

"Good. Also, do you speak Spanish?"

"Ah, no. Just some Gaelic and Japanese."

"Oh, are you mixed?"

Nova laughed lightly. She was used to the assumption. "Nah, white bread through and through."

"You don't look it."

"I know. Mum said we took after the dark Celts. All black hair and tanned skin and the like."

Frenchie nodded as if that was absolutely fascinating to her. And who knew, maybe it was. "Dark Celts? Huh, I think I wanna draw you someday. I'll tell the others you don't know Spanish then. I'll be back in about fifteen."

"Uh... okay?"

The thin girl gave a nod and then walked off with purpose. Come to think of it, Frenchie was looking more athletic and less underweight since the first time that Nova had met her. Sure, she didn't have Elizabeth levels of carved biceps, or even remotely close to Teddy's mechanic muscles, but she definitely seemed more... filled out. There was a story there, for sure.

But Nova didn't have much time to worry about it. Another group came up asking for some bread and real food, so she recited what Mum Miller had told her about the confections all being outside while refrigerated items were in through the food pantry's door. The whole exchange was quite polite, but by the time it was over, Nova had forgotten all about Frenchie and the children she had mentioned.

Or at least she did until the young woman returned, three others huddled close to her and another holding onto her arm with what looked like a death-grip even from a distance.

The death-grip one was a taller, lanky girl with sandy blond hair and a pleasant smattering of freckles on her pale face. Her eyes were shifting everywhere, from one side to the other, as if she was expecting an attack at any moment. Nova couldn't help but wonder what could have possibly put such a look of fear on the girl's face, her heart aching to smooth out those lines of terror and wrap the young thing right up in the fuzziest blanket.

The others behind Frenchie looked less terrified but still uncomfortable. There was a truly thin boy with dark skin and big glasses, his shoulders hunched in, a small girl who looked like she could be Frenchie's younger clone, and a heavier set young woman with deep circles under her eyes and her brown hair wild around her head.

"Like I was saying, this is one of my good people," Frenchie said, approaching the table. "You don't have to worry about Nova. She helps Lizzy take care of the animals on the ranch."

"Except never call Elizabeth that to her face," Nova added quickly, surprised that Frenchie remembered her name. They'd really only met in passing once. Maybe twice? "She's particular like that."

"Whoa, an accent," the thin boy remarked, shoving his glasses back up to where they'd slipped to rest at the bottom of his royal, broad nose. "Like the guy in the police box."

A laugh bubbled up out of Nova, surprised at the reference from the young man. He couldn't be much older than fifteen. "Exactly like that," she said when her mirth tapered off. "I have mostly baked goods out here, take whatever you like, and I can explain anything if you have questions. If you're looking for canned goods or perishables, like meat and produce, that can be found inside. We have two employees in every section of the food pantry, so there will always be someone around if you need help. Most of our volunteers are female." She added that last part ad-libbed, just on a theory, and that suspicion was confirmed when Death-grip's shoulders relaxed a little.

"I don't wanna go in," she whispered, her eyes darting up to Nova for only a moment before flicking back down.

"That's alright, Tawny. You don't have to. Why don't you stay right here and talk to Nova while Jules, Mac, and I head in?"

Tawny chewed at her lip, and Nova did her best to look non-threatening. After what felt like several full minutes, Death-grip nodded and the others filed off, still looking quite nervous.

"Are you a fan of sweets?" Nova asked when the young woman just stood there a while, hugging herself. There were signs along her arms, neck, and face of a rough life. Whether it was silver-white scars against her skin, discolorations, or darker marks, they spoke of someone who went without for long periods of time.

"Yeah... they're okay."

"Well, you should be able to find something you like here then. We have cake, cookies, a lil' bit of pie left. And of course, some regular loaves. But those are boring, sensible loaves, and you look like someone who could use a sugar high."

There it was, only for a second, but the tiniest of smiles made its way onto her lips before quickly fading. "You got any pecan pie?"

"Do I have pecan pie?" Nova said with a mock-huff. "What kind of respectable bake-sale lady would I be without a couple of slices of pecan pie?"

"...it's not a bake-sale, everything's free." Ah, again, just a sliver of character and a nano-second of a smile. Small things, but Nova knew first-hand how those things built up.

"Eh, semantics. Anyway, they're in the cooler underneath the table so they don't melt. Lemme get you some." She narrowed her eyes. "You look like a classic whip cream girl. Am I right?"

Tawny's eyes widened. "You got whipped cream?"

Nova nodded and proceeded to get out everything she needed. A few moments later, a slice was in Tawny's hands and she looked much less like she was going to bolt at any moment.

"I ain't starvin', ya know."

It seemed to come out of nowhere, and Nova looked up from the cooler she had opened up again to get herself a bottle of water.

"Come again?"

"I mean, I used to be, but then Frenchie helped me out. I got it okay now, meals on the regular. But uh, I guess... some habits are hard to break. Don't know how to make no desserts and buying them in the store seems too expensive."

Nova knew exactly what she meant. It had taken herself a full month of paychecks before she felt comfortable splurging on red meat in the supermarket. And Nova had only been dirt poor and on her own since she was nineteen. She could only guess at Tawny's story.

"Ah, that why Frenchie brought you here? To remind you about the sweeter things in life?"

"No... she wants me to not always have to be afraid if I gotta pass through this part of town."

"Not... afraid?"

That awful, crumpled look crossed her face. "A bad thing happened to me here."

Wait, what? Suddenly Nova's senses all went to high alert. "Are you okay? Do you need to leave? Was this recently?" She

knew it was too many questions too fast, but the whole situation had changed on a dime and she needed to *protect* the
young woman in front of her. It was written into her bones.

"No, no, it was a while ago. A couple years. It's just... still
hard. Frenchie says this place changed a lot and she doesn't
want me to have to be haunted by it, but she said she'd wait
until I was ready. Even if that was never."

"But you're here now, so it must not have been never."

Tawny nodded slowly, taking several bites of her pie.
"Frenchie is good people. She saved my life. If she wants me to
do something she thinks might help me, well, I figured I might
as well try."

Nova nodded along, her alarm fading. It seemed that she
was witnessing a happy part of the story, even if it clearly
hadn't been up to that point. "Well, I'm glad you're here. Someone's gotta eat all this pecan pie before it goes bad."

"Don't lie," Tawny shot right back, eyes narrowing. "You
hid that in the cooler so you could take it all home for
yourself."

The joke was so out of left field considering their previous
topic of conversation that Nova couldn't help but laugh again.
Goodness, she'd been smiling so much recently that she was
going to get face lines. And she didn't mind that one bit.

"Ag, you caught me. And here I thought I was going to get
away with it."

"I mean, I would do the same thing so..."

"...so you want another piece of pie?"

"Well, I certainly ain't complaining about that idea."

Nova went to serve her up another piece, and it was like
she'd won Tawny's trust. The young woman never fully *relaxed*,
but she did open up and her shoulders settled even more.

They had a fun conversation, one that continued when Frenchie and the others came out, each carrying a loaded bag. There was a kind lecture for Mac—the chubbier young woman—and Tawny from Frenchie as the artist explained that they both had jobs and needed to do better on feeding themselves quality, fresh items, and do less hoarding of canned goods and processed foods. Nova only chimed in where appropriate and otherwise just did her best to be a positive force for the nervous trio. By the time they left with Frenchie, all three of them were smiling and Nova felt wonderfully useful.

She could get addicted to the feeling, to be honest. It was so nice how it bubbled through her and made her feel validated. For once in her life she was doing real, tangible *good*. It was hard not to get swept up in the wonder of that, even with the sun beating down on her from overhead and her feet hurting from standing so much. She *could* sit, but in a way, she felt too excited and full of energy to do so.

"My oh my, I'm getting much too old for this!" Mum Miller said, finally rejoining the table and plopping herself onto one of the chairs. She was red-faced and her normally well-coifed hair was frizzy and loose around her head. Her braided bun had shaken loose from how she pinned it, going all the way down her back and revealing just how long it was.

"I don't know—I always like to think it's not how old you are, but how you are old," Nova quipped, reaching into the cooler for another water bottle only to realize that she'd already drunk the last one.

"Are you calling me old, darling?"

It was such an echo of Sal's statement that Nova's mind shot back to the muscled man. He was helping inside of the food pantry, in the back behind the counter where all the fridges were, but she'd still caught glimpses of him. He gave her all the space he promised her, and the few times their eyes had met, he'd given her a weak smile. No glower, no resentment.

It was becoming easier to accept his apology with each passing minute. He really did seem contrite.

"We're out of drinks," Nova said, sidestepping Mum Miller's verbal trap. "Is there a place where I can get you some cool ones?" Nova knew where to grab other ones to refill the coolers, just beside the food pantry where they were out of the way, but those would be very warm, and Nova *hated* drinking warm water or sports drinks. Gross.

"Oh, I think Sal stocked the fridge from the staff-kitchen at the back of the church. Should be able to grab some there. Thank you, sweetie, you're so thoughtful."

"Just want to make sure you don't pass out on me. It's hot today."

"If you think this is hot, you should have been here for twenty-eleven. That was a *real* scorcher." She kicked off her shoes and settled further into the chair. "Not that I'm asking for it back, or anything like that. Say..." she gave Nova a curious look. "How old were you even in 2011?"

Nova also knew that was a trap too, but a fun one. "I was twelve."

"*Twelve*? Good Lord, all of you keep getting younger and younger while my back never stops aging. Sal was right about... just graduating high school, I think? His birthday falls late in the year, so he was always younger than the rest of his class."

"He was seventeen," Nova answered after her brain did the automatic math.

"You came up with that answer mighty fast," Mum Miller said in a way that was clearly pleased.

"What drinks do you want?"

Thankfully, Mrs. Miller let the dodge happen and gave a general list of things she wouldn't mind, and Nova raced off. The walk around the massive church actually took a handful of minutes, and once she was inside, the wash of the AC over her was like a kiss of cooling refreshment.

Of course, her mind snapped to Sal again and she shook her head. Maybe she needed to not think about kisses for a while. Because the more time that her shock over the unre-quested kiss faded, the more her brain supplied *nicer* details about the experience.

Ugh.

Part of her wished that Sal had just *asked her* to go on a date or something. He was handsome and funny, and she had felt herself being drawn to him just as much as she wanted to draw him into the light. Why did he have to go and make everything so messy?

Nova sighed to herself and made her way to the staff kitchen, enjoying the way her skin was prickling under the conditioned air. Even with her shorts and tank top—with a generous helping of sunscreen—she was still fairly sweaty from being outside for several hours. If she was in her normal jumpsuit, she was pretty sure she would have right about died.

Thankfully, she didn't get lost, remembering where the kitchen was from her earlier tour to the bathroom before their morning had really swung into gear. There were all sorts of snacks on the counter, and several more cases of drinks stacked to the side of the fridge. The great thing about the mega-church seemed to be that it had mega-space to keep all the volunteers healthy, hydrated, and full of energy.

Pulling the fridge door open, she grabbed one of the cloth bags hanging from a hook and loaded it up with drinks. She got the lemonade-tea mix—although she still maintained that American tea was an abomination half the time—that Mum Miller wanted, some extra water bottles, some sports drinks, and a couple of sodas. She knew that everyone had to go careful on the soft drinks considering they could dehydrate, but it was plenty easy to sweat out a bunch of electrolytes and get desalinated. As long as it was balanced with water, it would be okay for folks to have a bottle during the day.

When she was done loading up, the bag was considerably heavy, and she grunted as she hauled it onto her shoulder. Taking a deep breath to head back out into the heat, she took a step towards the door.

She didn't quite get there before it swung open, surprising her. Yelping, she jumped back only for the momentum of her bag to make her stumble. For a moment she was sure that her knee was going to do *the thing*, but she managed to regain her balance without any drama.

Whew, it looked like her luck was really changing. It was about time.

"Whoa, you okay there?"

Nova looked up to see a young woman and two young men had entered. None of them looked very sweaty or sun-soaked, so she guessed either they were working in the food pantry or they were some of the young folk who volunteered to clean the church and water the plants during their college breaks. Something about building character and fellowship; Nova had only been half-listening on her tour to the bathroom, the need to relieve herself after her morning coffee had been awful distracting.

"I'm fine. Just gave me a good startle. I always hate when that happens."

"Yeah," the girl said. But her tone wasn't nearly as pleasant as Nova's. Not that it was hostile. It just was... well, it made a curl of suspicion wiggle its way up Nova's spine. "You're one of the volunteers outside, right? From the Miller ranch?"

"Yeah. Was just grabbing drinks. I should head out." She said it with a smile on her face, sure that she was being needlessly alarmist, but the three made a sort of informal blockage between her and the exit. It didn't seem purposeful, and yet...

"You one of them gays?" the largest of the young men asked, a smile on his face.

"Huh? No," Nova answered quickly, so surprised by the out of nowhere question that she answered without thinking. "Not that I think it matters right now, either way. I need to get back; Mum Miller is thirsty."

"You sure? Cause, you know." He gestured to his own head; finger pinched close together. "Because of the hair thing."

"You can't tell if someone's gay by their haircut. That's ridiculous." She wasn't about to explain that the south was incredibly hot for her after growing up in the UK and also that her pixie cut emphasized her cheekbones in a way that made her feel statuesque.

"You one of those feminists then? Surprised the Millers would hire that. But my dad says they've been straying ever since their son rolled around here and started accusing folks in the ministry of insane things."

"I don't know what you're talking about," Nova said shortly. She was done. She was *so* done. Part of her wanted to haul off and tell them what she really thought, tearing their obviously overinflated egos to itty bitty shreds, but she didn't want to mess up the occasion for Solomon, Mrs. Miller, and all of the hungry people who were getting treats that they normally didn't have access to.

But she was *sorely* tempted.

"Is that a tattoo?" the girl asked, pointing down.

Nova looked to the bottom of her shorts where just the curled tail of a bearded dragon was sticking out. Her bottoms went a couple of inches below her fingertips, but they were shorter than the ones she had worn when baking with Sal, revealing a tiny bit of the tattoo she'd gotten when she first moved out of her parents' house. It was a sign of freedom, of unabashedly embracing one of the "weird" things that she loved.

"Yes," was her clipped reply.

"You know you're going to hell, right?"

What? Before Nova's brain could even process why someone would think that God would object to something as simple as ink on skin, the girl kept talking.

"You know, if you're going to volunteer for a church, you should really dress your best instead of showing up in inappropriate rags."

There was only so much that Nova could tolerate, and they were squarely beyond it. "Alright, this has been fun and all, but I've got some work to do. Goodbye."

Nova went to push past them, aiming between the smaller man and the girl, both of who she had several inches on. She was almost out the door when someone gripped her wrist, jerking her back. The bag on her shoulder made her miss a step, and when she righted herself, she saw it was the biggest one gripping her.

Nova wasn't much of one for physical fighting. She didn't enjoy hurting people, and it wasn't a natural instinct to her. But she twisted her wrist sharply and yanked her hand down then up rapidly, popping it out of the man's grip like her friend had taught her back on the base in the UK. But the movement was so jerky that she managed to knock the guy in the chin, leaving a stabbing point of pain in the top of her hand. That was going to hurt the next day.

"*Ow,*" she hissed to herself, shaking her hand. But then she realized the guy was retaliating, his hand pulled back into a fist.

She tried to recall what her friend tried to teach her to defend herself, but her arms just flew up, crossed to protect her head. Her heart was pounding, and her stomach was lurching. Despite her frame, she wasn't one for battle. Sure, she could out-strength a lot of people, but that didn't mean she knew how to throw a punch or deflect one. Suddenly she found herself wishing she had listened more to her friend who wanted her to be able to defend herself and rely less on her loud voice and sharp glares to intimidate people.

She braced, fearing the worst, her mind going to how the three could hurt her and how they could get away with it. It would be her word versus theirs. They could say she came onto the girl, or that she was stealing. And maybe Mum Miller wouldn't believe it, maybe none of the Millers would, but what could they do against a whole church of mega-rich folks? Surely, they wouldn't be willing to risk their social and political positions for her, some poor girl from the UK who had already chastised one of their sons?

But the hit never landed. There was a rush of air behind her, then something moving past her, then the sounds of a scuffle. Cracking open her eyes, she couldn't quite believe what she saw.

And yet there he was, Sal, standing in the kitchen with the punching guy by the back of his shirt collar, glaring at the other two. He looked absolutely *terrifying*, like some sort of dark avenger from a movie, all rippling muscles and lethal glower.

"You all want to tell me what happened here?"

His voice was low, dangerous, and it was the so-far-silent man who spoke.

"She was steal—"

Sal gave the biggest one a good rattle, then shoved him towards his friends.

"Try again."

"We—"

"You know what, never mind. I don't care who you think you all are or who your parents are, you do not put your hands on someone else without permission? Do you understand?"

"Look, Silas—"

"I'm *Salvatore,*" he bit harshly, practically baring his teeth at the group. "You know, the *angry* Miller brother." Finally, he looked to her and some of the intensity of his face eased. "Are you alright? Do they need to say anything to you?"

"I just want them gone," Nova answered shakily. Sure, maybe an apology would be called for, but she was still shaky from all the adrenaline. She would have fought back if he'd hit her, but it would have been sloppy and helter-skelter. She didn't even want to think what the result of that would have been if Sal hadn't shown up.

"You heard the lady," Sal snapped, gesturing towards the door. "Get out of here. Before I think better of it."

The three quickly hurried out, and Nova didn't know whether to cry or hug Sal. He saved her. He didn't even know what they had been saying, or if she had antagonized them. He'd seen her about to be hurt and he'd stood up for her.

"Are you alright? Did they hurt you?" he took a cautious

step towards her, his hands held up again nonthreateningly. "Nova?"

Perhaps it was hypocritical given everything that had happened, but suddenly her mind seemed to decide on both reactions at the same time. A relieved sob bubbled up from between her lips at the same time her arms went out to cling tightly to Sal's muscled frame in a hug.

Nobody had *ever* stood up for her like that.

21

Salvatore

*O*h.

So many things had happened so quickly that Sal was still scrambled by it. He'd been heading in to use the bathroom and wash his hands—after accidentally grabbing some meat that hadn't been packaged properly—when he'd heard some snide voices.

For a moment he'd intended to ignore it, but then he heard someone who sounded like Nova, although it wasn't exactly easy to tell considering how short and clipped the responses were. He'd headed over and opened the door out of curiosity. The last thing he'd expected was for Nova to be recoiling as a man who was bigger than her readied a punch.

The part right after that was a blur. Sal knew he'd seen red, and he'd rushed forward to put a stop to any of that. The thought of anyone putting their hands on Nova, on trying to *hurt* her, made his blood pulse in his ears. He never wanted her to wear that same shocked, horrified expression she'd had when he'd kissed her without permission, never wanted her to feel small or vulnerable.

A moment later, he'd been yelling at the attackers and then ordering them out once Nova said she wanted them gone. Some part of him itched for him to do more, to make sure they *never* hurt anyone again, but if Nova didn't want that, then he wouldn't indulge the temptation.

He'd approached her, just wanting to make sure she was okay, when she'd lunged forward and *hugged* him.

Except hug didn't really do it justice. It was like she was holding onto him for dear life, her face pressed into his chest. He could tell through the thin fabric of his shirt that there were wet tears trying to run down her face only to get absorbed by the cotton.

He moved slowly, a bit in shock, but let his arms circle around her as well. That seemed to comfort her, and she practically melted into his chest, her hands clutching the fabric of his shirt with slightly less desperation.

Wow.

A simple embrace shouldn't make him feel like his heart was going to explode at any moment, and yet there he was, Nova's arms wrapped around him, crying against him.

It would have been easy to get lost in that sensation, or even let it be at the forefront of his mind. But as warm and alluring as it was, it took a backseat to her wellbeing. She was crying. He'd seen Nova dislocate her knee multiple times, then force it into place, and she'd never so much as shed a tear.

"Hey, I'm here. I'm right here."

She said something, but it was muffled by his chest and her hiccupping sobs.

"What was that?" he asked.

Nova peeled her face away from him, the damp spot of his shirt sticking to his skin.

"I'm sorry," she said. Her arms came down and she wiped her face, rubbing the tears away as if she was angry with them.

"Sorry for what?"

"I yelled at you before about touching me without permission, and now I just hugged you without warning. Seems hypocritical."

"Two very different situations. But you're allowed to hug me as long as you need. What happened? Are you alright?" It was probably the fourth time that he had asked that, but he couldn't help it. He was worried.

"Yeah, I was just surprised, angry, and maybe a little scared. Goes right to my tear ducts."

She shifted, bending slightly to grab a heavy bag that she had dropped. Sal reached for it on instinct, hauling it up for her.

"Can we get out of here?" she asked with so much exhaustion lacing her tone that it tugged at his heart.

"Of course. Whatever you want."

To his surprise, she hooked her arm through his free one, tucking herself into his side. She kept her gaze pointed exactly forward, never deviating as they made their way outside and onto the back steps. There she stopped, sitting down and heaving another long sigh.

Sal didn't know what to do. Part of him was furious for whatever those teens had done to bother Nova, another part of him was worried about what was going on with the normally unrufflable woman. And then yet another part wondered if he should go. But she *had* said she had forgiven him, and the thought of leaving her alone when she was so upset made his skin itch.

Pulling his phone from his pocket, he texted his mother that he and Nova needed a break then sat right next to her. Reaching into the heavy bag, he handed her one of the sports drinks and took a bottle of water for himself. Maybe the electrolytes and sugars would make her feel better. Sal himself hadn't cried in a long while, but that didn't mean he had forgotten how awful it always made him feel.

"Thanks," she said, sipping at it, her chin in her hand as she stared into the distance.

That same mix of fury and concern twisted in Sal's gut. He wanted to make it all better. Make *her* feel better.

"For everything," she finished after a several minute pause. "I think... I think it might have been bad if you hadn't shown up."

Sal made a sound of agreement. "You know, my brother warned me to make sure that you and Frenchie never were alone inside of the church. At first I thought he was being overprotective—he gets that about her sometimes—but now I get it. I'm thinking this place, and a lot of these people, aren't as great as I thought they were."

"They're like what I mentioned before, I think," Nova said slowly.

She blinked and shook her head slightly, her gaze seeming to clear. That gave Sal hope. It couldn't have been so bad if she was already recovering... right?

She continued, "People who are supposed to love like Jesus but have gotten so sidetracked by money and hate that they don't even realize they've set themselves up with false idols."

Sal didn't say anything to that, turning over her words in his mind. Was that what they were like? Was that what his family was like? The megachurch was sponsored specifically by his family, full of business partners and other folks in their social circles. What did it mean when some of the parishioners kept doing things that were about as far from Jesus-like as one could get?

"I'm fine, you know. It wasn't a big deal. You can go back to work if you want."

"I don't mind sitting here a few more moments, should you want me. But if you want to be alone, I can—"

"No!" she cut him off hastily, her cheeks coloring pink slightly. "Uh, that's alright. I'd rather not be alone right now."

"Then I don't mind sitting."

Because he didn't. Not at all. He was happy to plant his butt on that stone step until it went numb. That same companionable silence settled between them, the background noise of the food pantry barely registering. It was lovely, despite the awful way that it had started, and Sal found himself closing his eyes.

Why was it he felt so contented whenever he was by Nova? The insecurity, the need to impress people, it all fell to the back of his head, just leaving the moment. It was something that he hadn't even known was possible, and yet that was the only way to describe the peace he felt near her.

Well... peace and then a whole lot of attraction.

He kept his eyes to respectable places, but it was impossible not to notice how well her outfit fit her, and the strength and length of her legs. Her tanned skin was already darkened from her morning in the sun, despite all the sunscreen he'd seen her put on, and some freckles were growing more prominent across her nose. She was a vision, the perfect juxtaposition of sharp angles and strong features combined with a sort of curvy softness that some women seemed to just have.

Sal was aware that Nova wasn't perhaps what everyone thought of when their minds conjured up a beautiful woman, but she was undeniably that to him. And it was a radiant sort of look, one that glowed from within her, making it seem like she shined whenever he looked at her. He truly didn't understand how someone like her ended up poor, alone, and working as a vet tech assistant on his family's ranch.

She took another long sip of her drink, and Sal's gaze went to her full lips. He tried not to think about those, he did, but it was hard not to. As ashamed as he was about that kiss, as *bad* as he felt about crossing her boundaries and only thinking about himself, he still couldn't forget how incredible that kiss had felt.

The kiss had been completely different from anything he'd experienced in college, or on any of the few short relationships he'd tried since then when he got bored. She was so *soft*, so perfect that it had filled up all of his senses and left him reeling.

Too bad it had been a stolen kiss. How much nicer would it have been if she was ready for it? If she was just as enthusiastic and desired him as much as he did her?

That was a dangerous line of thought, and Sal banished it from his mind. Besides, he was pretty sure he had ruined that with his behavior that fateful afternoon. He'd known he'd messed up, but he hadn't *really* gotten it until Silas and Sterling had spelled so much out for him. How Nova probably didn't know if he was going to try to punish her for rejecting him. Or worse. That she was probably scared that he might try to push it farther, demand things that it wasn't right for anyone to demand. Sal had been shocked by the idea and resisted that she could even think that was a possibility, but the twins had shared just some of the stories that Teddy and

Elizabeth had told them over the months that they were dating.

Insane. The world was insane, and the thought that Nova had been worried that he could be like that made him sick. The thought that it happened often enough that it was a possible thing in the world made him even sicker. It was right about then that he realized that something had to change.

"You know, I've been thinking about what you told me," he said after the silence dragged on again.

"Hmm?" she asked, blinking and craning her neck to look at him.

He lowered himself another step so she wouldn't have to twist so much, and she sent him a grateful smile that made his heart go off-rhythm for a moment.

"About what you said," he repeated.

"I'm sorry, mate, but I say a whole lot of things."

He cracked a grin at that. Even when she was stressed to the gills, Nova still had her dry wit. "About all the resources my family and I have. You're right, it's not like we're hurting for anything, so I don't see how I can just sit around and not try to change things."

"*Oh.*"

She certainly seemed surprised by his statement, but the brightness that traveled across his features made him feel perhaps more full of pride than it should. Oh well, something to deal with later.

"So you've seen your brothers' way of thinking?"

"Well, I don't know about all *that*. I'm still trying to fit in what they say along with what I thought the world was, and I'm still not sure where my father is wrong and where they are. But I'm listening. And I *do* think that we don't need to worry ourselves with profits as much. I think we need to focus more on what we're doing for the world than always concerning ourselves with trying to snatch as much out of it as possible."

"That sounds like a good start."

"Yeah. But it's only a start. I've got a lot of sorting to do still. I guess you could say that I've done a whole lot of thinking this past week."

"Have you?"

Sal nodded. "The whole thing that happened between you and me, and then the talk I had with my brothers, made me stop and think on why... everything shook down like it did."

"You talked to your brothers?"

Another nod. Sal hoped that she wouldn't be upset by that. "I needed someone I trusted to help me work through everything that was going on with my mind, and the twins seemed like the best bet."

"So, you trust the twins?"

"That seems to be the case."

Finally, she smiled, a real smile, the corners of her eyes crinkling. "I'm very happy to hear that. You know, if you're still sorting and thinking and all that, why don't you follow me around at work come Monday? Just to see how much the animals' lives have improved and see where that leaves you in your, uh, sorting process. Additional data and all that. Maybe you could even meet some of the other workers."

There was that thump in his chest again, one of excitement, but also of fear. The chance to be close with Nova, to banter with her again, to spend an entire day or more just being in her presence was all pretty appealing. What was not appealing was the thought of disappointing her.

And yet he agreed anyway, a smile of his own breaking out. Maybe with her help, he could prove that he was good for something besides his muscles.

22

Nova

*I*f someone had told Nova when she'd started her new job that a billionaire heir was going to end up following her around, listening to her and nodding at her like she was his supervisor, she would have called them crazy. And yet for a whole solid week, Sal had been shadowing her.

There were a few odd looks from it, sure, but she didn't mind. She explained things when she needed to, but for the most part, the workers on the ranch seemed to know not to question the sudden changes in behavior that the Miller sons seemed apt to suddenly go through.

Sal was quiet most of the time, those handsome brows of his usually furrowed in concentration. The good thing was that he asked questions most of the time when he seemed particularly perplexed, and would occasionally write something down in a tiny notebook he kept in his jeans pocket.

And *goodness*, did the man look cut out of an art book when he wore those classic, dark washed work jeans that his older brothers favored. The man was definitely rocking the look. Which was probably disrespectful to think, but when God had carved out the diagram for Sal, he hadn't exactly been playing fair.

She kept that to herself, however. If Sal was trusting her to teach him, to lead him on his information-gathering journey so he could figure out how he was going to help the world, then she could keep her rude thoughts to herself.

But still... did he have to be just so... *sculpted*?

That question remained unanswered, however, but that was just about the only one. Nova did her best to make sure she gave Sal whatever info he needed, and when she didn't know, she found out. And when she thought there was something he should know that he didn't think to ask for, she got right on that too.

So naturally, on Monday morning and the beginning of week two in their little shadowing setup, when Nova found out that he didn't know a single worker by name, she went about introducing him to every single one that she could find.

Which was quite a lot.

Thankfully, Elizabeth had long since given her blessing as long as Nova kept her phone on loud enough to hear emergency calls, so she didn't have to worry about falling behind in her work. Besides, despite all the extra time it took to bring Sal up to speed, it turned out that having a giant of a man always with her to help her with tasks had actually gotten her ahead of where she and Elizabeth had planned. Especially since they were able to take two horses on a walk instead of one, Filbert the gelding joining Amaranth on needing gentle, physical therapy trots around the ranch.

"Your brain leaking out of your ears yet?" Nova asked with a laugh as they hopped into the golf cart that they'd pulled up to the employee lunch building in. She tried not to chuckle as she watched Sal fold himself up to fit inside. It really was comical given just how *big* he was, but also endearing, in a way.

"Is that what that feeling is?" he asked with that same sort of curled smile that always made her stomach flip.

In some ways she hated that she was so affected by him, but the more time they spent together, the more she stopped resisting it.

"Yup. But the more you practice and get to know folks, the more those names will stick around."

He nodded as she drove along in their usual companionable silence. Nova liked to talk, but there was something calming about being with Sal while he was digesting ideas and ruminating. Like she could see the wheels turning inside of his mind and how he was growing with each new thing that he had decided.

Suddenly an idea came to her. "Hey, you mentioned that your mom packed you a lunch basket today, right?"

"Yeah," he said with plenty of chagrin. "She's mighty pleased that I'm spending so much time with you and out on the ranch. Said I needed to get out of the house because I was turning into a ghost."

"She's pleased about us hanging out together?" Nova said, her cheeks flushing. Just like there was something about Sal that made her heart race sometimes, there was something about Mum Miller that made Nova feel so safe. She had a warmth to her, that woman, and Nova couldn't help but wonder if she would be different if she'd had a mum as kind as the Miller matriarch.

"That's the impression I got. Better be careful, next time you're in the manor, she might lock you in and keep you there."

Nova did laugh at that, the warmth in her belly spreading even more throughout her body. "I wasn't sure if she hadn't already done that with Frenchie." Nova gave him a sort of sidelong look. "I have to ask you a question."

"Uh-huh?"

"Did you really call Frenchie the *French Woman* when you were first explaining things to me."

Sal shifted slightly, ducking his head, which certainly was a sight to see in the golf cart. "...maybe."

"Salvatore Miller, Frenchie is *Latina* and *American*."

"I mean, her name is Frenchie, can you blame me for the assumption?" His tone was playful as much as it was abashed.

Goodness, he was cute.

"Her name is *Francesca*."

"...right. I knew that."

"Uh-huh, I'm sure you did." She laughed at his contrite grin, shaking her head. The days were shifting into shorter ones, fall slowly sweeping in, but her days seemed brighter than ever. "You want to take that lunch and go sit by the horse stables? Elizabeth cleared it, but most of the horses are spending their time outside anyway."

"Yeah, that sounds nice."

Nova nodded and changed the direction of the golf cart while Sal continued speaking, his voice a low rumble that sat just right with her.

"You know, I haven't gone to my cousins' ranch in ages, but they've got these gorgeous hills that overlook several parts of their property. One of them is even in a treelike grove. I wish you could see it."

"Well, why not arrange a visit?"

Oh no, that was awfully assumptive. Nova tried not to squirm in her seat, but Sal didn't even seem to notice.

"Unfortunately, I don't exactly know if we're welcome."

"Why, what happened?"

"Well, my youngest brother, Simon, announced that he was going to go backpacking around the world for six months last year and a family fight broke out."

"Oh."

"Yeah, so we're not on the best terms. I haven't seen my brother, Samuel, in a couple years."

"Wait, I thought it was Simon who went abroad."

"It was. Samuel is my eldest brother, who left our ranch to permanently live with our aunt and uncle. Even found himself a fiancée."

"Huh," Nova's mind scrambled for a moment to connect all the dots. "You know, this would all be a lot easier if your names didn't all start with 'S.'"

"Sorry, Miller tradition. The mothers pick a letter and stick with it for all their children. Been happening for generations. My uncle goes by his middle name, though. Apparently, Maximillian didn't fit him like McLintoc fit my dad."

Nova felt her eyes snap open even wider at that. "Your uncle's name is *Maximillian*?"

"Yup," he said, popping the "p" at the end before laughing himself. "It doesn't fit him at all. My uncle says about four words a year, and he's about as homeboy as you can get. Real hands-on and rustic. My dad calls him a bleeding heart. Goes back to an old rift from years before I was born, apparently."

Well if that didn't explain a whole lot. Nova wished she could meet these Miller cousins, but she also wondered if she could handle being surrounded by that many wealthy, hand-some ranchers at once.

"I see. Surely it was an argument about which of your family branches inherited the most dashing genes."

"You think we're dashing?" Sal shot back in what was quickly becoming a repeated joke between them.

"Hush now, don't get distracted."

"I'd rather be distracted than have to answer if my cousins are hot or not."

Nova didn't say anything to that, enjoying her quiet mirth at the whole exchange. But then Sal kept on.

"...yeah, they are. Unfairly handsome, the lot of them. Used to be real jealous when I was younger."

The moment of honesty wasn't expected, but it was appreciated. Nova always felt so trusted, so *important* whenever he was vulnerable in front of her. Especially because she got the impression that it wasn't easy for him.

They made it to the stables, and he pulled the small cooler from the back, also surprising her by unrolling a throw blanket. She wasn't quite sure where he'd gotten it, but she certainly wasn't complaining as he laid it out for her to sit on.

The lunch was simple enough, but lovely and filling, perfect for a late summer day complete with a thermos of sweet lemonade. They chewed and drank at it casually, watching the horses as they did their things, and Nova thought she might actually be content.

"You know, I've been thinking this past week," Sal said.

"That's good, kinda the whole point of this shadowing thing."

He flicked a piece of cucumber from his sandwich at her, and she responded by picking it off her cheek and eating it. He rolled his eyes at her, which made her feel unusually bubbly.

Goodness, if he knew half of what went on inside of her, he would think she was insane.

"*Anyway*, I've been thinking, and I've realized some stuff."

Oh! It was serious time. Nova turned her attention away from the bright, snappy feeling and settled down to listen. "What kind of stuff?"

"Well... it's not really easy to look in the mirror and see everything you've been doing wrong, but I think that's where I'm at. The more I see, the more I talk to my brothers, the more time I spend with *you*, the more I realize how much my family has messed up.

"We've caused a whole lot of pain. Probably more than I know. It goes beyond the workers or even the animals. Even the people that my father has been trying to get elected don't always have the best interest of the public in mind."

"Like?"

"Well, you know, help for the poor, more equality, more resources for people who need it. It doesn't make sense for my family to have more money than we could ever spend while some folks don't even come close to reaching the poverty line. Like Jesus said, it's harder for a rich man to get into heaven than it is to pass through the eye of a needle, and the way it looks right now, it's like we ain't even tried."

Nova could swear that her heart was glowing, each word out of Sal's mouth sounding like it was thoroughly thought over. It meant so much that he'd come to those conclusions on his own. Sure, she'd introduced him to some new ideas, and new people, encouraged him to have conversations that he might not have otherwise, but really, the revelations were all his own.

"I've been, I dunno, listless I suppose you can say. For a long time. I've been chasing my father's approval, trying to carve out a place for myself, but I realize that's not what I want to do."

"What do you want to do?" If it were anyone else, she would swear that Sal was just saying what she wanted to hear him say, but she trusted him. Despite his misstep, he had always been honest and upfront with her. Even when he didn't like her at all.

"On the grand scale? I'm not sure yet. But I know I need to do *something*. Solomon has the food pantry and the work he does in the city with Frenchie. Silas has the community center, while Sterling has the soil amendment experiment and all of the animal shenanigans.

"I need something of my own, to work hard and struggle and pour all of my effort into. I want to be able to change people's lives, because you're right, I really have the resources to do *something*. Even if I don't know what that something is yet."

Nova felt like if she smiled any harder, her cheeks would start to throb. "I'm excited to hear what you come up with. And I'd be happy to be your sounding board if you need someone to bounce ideas off."

"Of course. If there's one thing I can always rely on you for—"

"It's an opinion," Nova finished for him with a cackle that was probably too loud, but she didn't care. "Now, what about on the everyday scale? You said that you weren't sure what you wanted to do on a grand scale, but that implies that you know what you want to do on the everyday scale."

"Ah. Right. Well..." He swallowed, and she watched his Adam's apple bob. "I want to be a better man. I want to let go of all these bad feelings I have inside of me. I want people to be happy to see me, to feel a sort of warmth when I enter a room. I want to be someone who's known for showing Jesus' love, not for being the son of a rich man who has more money than he could ever spend in a lifetime. Several lifetimes even." His eyes were far off in the distance as he spoke, which was probably a good thing, because if he was looking at her directly, Nova might have burst into tears.

He was just so *good*. Could he see it? That light flickering inside of him? The one that wanted to do right even if he didn't know exactly what that was.

"I want to be someone my mom can be proud of."

Nova understood that feeling more than anything else he said, and her heart squeezed in her chest. But unlike her own mum, she believed that Sal could absolutely be that for his mother. Mum Miller was a kind woman, full of love and light, and Nova wouldn't be surprised if she already was proud of her son in many, many ways.

It was so sweet, so honest and open that she was caught up in the rush of all of it. Turning, she went up onto her knees, her hands coming up to cup his face.

The expression on his face was so raw, so open as their gazes locked. He took in a shuddering breath that seemed to roll to her too, licking his lips before he spoke.

"What are you doing?" he asked, already sounding wrecked.

"I'm asking if I can kiss you right now," she answered. In any other moment, she might have been embarrassed at how breathless her voice was, but that was just about the last thing registering in her mind. She just knew that she was caught up in everything in her and going on with Sal. She was so *happy* for him.

"*Why?*"

He sounded surprised, uncertain, worried, maybe even hopeful.

"Because I want to," she answered honestly. Because goodness, did she *ever* want to kiss him. She craved it from the bottom of her feet right up to the top of her head. She needed to kiss him like she needed *air*.

But most importantly, she needed permission.

He looked at her, looked into the deepest parts of her, then he closed the distance.

He kissed her, his arms winding about her waist, so strong and secure.

It was a gentle kiss, tentative even. Nova wasn't exactly the most experienced with the act, but she followed his lead.

He held her just right. His closeness wasn't scary like it had been before but reassuring instead. She knew his hands were meant for protection, not harm. He'd proven that thrice over when he'd saved her at the church function.

They clung to each other, and Nova felt herself sinking into the haze of it all. Her body was warm, her blood was rushing, and she never wanted to stop feeling so wonderful.

She'd never felt so wanted, so welcome, and so desired. It was a rushing wave through her, and one it was so easy to drown in.

Too easy.

One of his hands moved to cup her face gently. Lovingly.

Clearing her throat, she broke away from the kiss, breath raspy. Sal pulled back, giving her a half-lidded look that made her want to go right back to kissing him silly.

"I'm getting carried away, aren't I?" he asked, his face flushing even deeper.

Nova felt a flash of pride that *she* was the one that had gotten him into such a state. She'd always been called ugly when she was younger. Too tall to be feminine, too skinny to be a woman, and then too fat to be desirable. Her personality was too brash, and her frame was too broad, and her hair was too short.

But when Sal looked at her, all of those other people didn't matter.

"I'm right there with you, mate."

"Right."

He sat back and looked at her. At least his breath was also rushed, his lips swollen slightly by their kissing. Nova wondered if she had stubble-burn on her cheeks or mouth. The idea made her toes curl happily in her work boots.

"Do you—" Sal started.

"Want to go on a date with me?" Nova blurted before he could finish whatever he was going to say.

Sal blinked at her a moment before a broad smile broke out across his face. "I was gonna suggest a walk to cool down, but I like your idea better."

"Yeah, well," Nova felt herself blushing, but she didn't let that trip her up. "Why not both?"

23

Salvatore

Sal wiped his hands on the side of his pants, his stomach doing something aerobatic that he wasn't exactly fond of. He'd stopped pacing the foyer for a moment but found himself doing that again after checking his phone.

He was off-kilter because Nova was the one who had arranged their whole date and was picking him up, but he was more than willing to go with her flow. Besides, it was kind of nice not to have to deal with the planning part. Goodness knew his head was plenty full of all the personal decisions he'd been coming to over the past two weeks.

Of course, Sal hadn't done any of it *for* Nova, but he couldn't lie that he was right pleased when she'd asked to kiss him, her eyes hazy and her tanned cheeks flushed pink. She'd looked so beautiful in that moment, so proud of him, and his heart had practically sung as their lips touched.

He wouldn't mind kissing her again, that was for certain, but all in good time. He wasn't in a rush.

...but he did wish Nova would hurry up and arrive.

It was awfully early, the sun still not due to set for a couple of hours, and it was right at four o'clock sharp when she pulled up to the front. Sal opened the door before she could even get fully out of her car, doing his best not to bound over to her.

"Oh, hey there," she said, offering her arms up with a grin. Sal stepped into them and let her hug him, wrapping his own arms around her and giving her a quick hug. It didn't last nearly as long as he would have liked, but when she stepped away, he took a moment to look her over.

She was wearing a dress, the first time that he had ever seen her in one. It was a pale blue gingham, kind of done in a retro style, shoulders bare so she could soak up the sun.

"You look good," he said, swallowing hard. She just batted her lashes at him and then opened the back of her car. "Where are we going, by the way. Are you going to tell me yet?"

"Actually," she backed out from where she'd bent into her car, pulling out a truly massive picnic basket complete with the checkered top. "I thought a summer-end picnic would be fun."

Sal grinned at her. She was just so cute, standing there in her pretty dress, holding her basket. "That sounds amazing."

She smiled back at him, and he realized that she was wearing makeup. Nothing too intense, but a dark eyeliner and pretty lipstick that drew his gaze down to her plush lips. He wondered, if he kissed her while she wore that, if he would end up with it smeared across his chin or if it was her face that would end up streaked with it.

Hmmm, he liked that idea more than he should, probably.

Then again, he was pretty excited for anything that led to kissing Nova, now that he knew the attraction between them was mutual.

Or at least he hoped it was. He didn't imagine Nova was the type to kiss someone without any sort of feelings for them. And he certainly didn't think she could kiss him like *that* if she wasn't at least a little drawn to him.

"Alright, let's walk then," she said, holding her arm out for him to hook his through it.

Sal carried the picnic basket while they walked together, no one to interrupt them with the skeleton crew that ran on the weekend. A skeleton crew that made three extra dollars an hour thanks to Solomon's new policies.

There wasn't a picturesque hill to perch on top of, but Nova led him to an open spot between the edge of their property and the barns. It was a space that was supposed to have something or other built on it for the animals, but at the moment none of that seemed to matter.

He spread out the blanket for Nova, putting the basket on one edge, and then sat down and patted the ground beside him. She sat down all ladylike beside him, covering her knees with her dress. Their bodies barely touching.

"Is this alright?" she asked, voice so soft.

He had no idea how it couldn't be, but still appreciated that she asked. "This is just about perfect."

"Only just about?"

"Well, I don't know what you've brought in that picnic basket."

"Nothing to get too excited about. I'm not a great cook like your mother."

She bent forward, grabbed the picnic basket, and placed it in front of them. Sal felt so warm and comfortable. It was the intimacy of being close with someone without anything sexual, just the appreciation of each other's presence.

Not that his mind didn't occasionally wander, such was human nature. He did his best to ignore those thoughts. Granted, that probably would have been a lot easier if he hadn't wandered into dangerous territory during college. But all those interactions seemed so shallow to him now.

As she opened up the basket, Sal found himself laughing, loud and unrestricted. Mostly because the first thing he saw was a truly massive chocolate cake.

"You didn't get enough of baking with my mom?" he heard himself ask.

"You get enough of eating sweets?"

"No, never." Although he was certainly going to need to ramp up his gym time.

"Then no, didn't get enough of baking then."

"So, is this a sort of sugar rush thing or..."

"Don't worry, I brought sandwiches too. Almond butter and jelly, then some deli-meat ones. Mum Miller told me those used to be your favorite." She gave him a saucy look as she hauled the kitchen baggies out that were indeed filled with sandwiches. "Should have known that you were too fancy for peanut butter, like a normal kid."

Sal just leveled her with his own deadpan expression. "Of all the words you might use to describe me, is normal anywhere on that list?"

"Fair enough."

She pulled out some paper plates then put the sandwiches on them, along with a small, personal bag of chips. It wasn't fancy, but it didn't need to be. It was thoughtful, and Sal realized he was hungrier than he had thought.

They ate together, the sun just beginning its descent to the west of the manor. It truly was beautiful, seeing a huge swath of their land lit up like that, and he just took it in. He couldn't remember the last time he'd watched that great ball of fire sink into the earth. Had to have been when he was a kid, back when he and his brothers would stay out well into the night and make bonfires out behind the house.

"This is nice," he said when he finished his food, taking the thermos that Nova handed to him. He unscrewed the lid and was surprised when what was unmistakably peach tea filled his mouth.

He swallowed the refreshing, cool drink then marveled at the woman in his lap. "You made—"

"The horrible abomination that is considered tea here? Yeah. I did," Nova answered with a grin. "Needless to say, I truly am a martyr."

"It actually tastes good, too."

She gave him a sharp look at that. "Excuse you, if I am going to defile all that is good and holy about tea, I'm at least going to do it *right*. Besides..." Her expression grew sheepish. "I had your mom teach me how."

She was too perfect, too cute. He found himself setting the thermos to the side and wrapped his arms around her, squeezing her into a hug. It was just tea, but it felt like so much more. It felt like she cared.

"Thank you," he said into her short, soft hair. "I love it."

"No problem," she murmured, melting right into him again. He loved how she did that too. She was so strong, so relentless, but she seemed to relax and meld into him like water sometimes. It made him feel... important? Was that the right word? He wasn't sure, but it seemed close enough. "How about some cake?"

He nodded, afraid to ruin the moment with his words, and

watched as she cut them two generous slices. He was surprised to see it was bright red inside, clearly moist, and somehow not sweating in the evening heat.

"Is that red velvet cake?"

She nodded. "Yeah, I tried really hard on the recipe. Although it's mostly just a ton of food coloring."

Sal didn't care how much food coloring it was. He held out his hands, making the grabby motion that never failed to get a laugh. And when she did laugh, it made his heart warm yet again.

That poor slice of cake never stood a chance, though, and neither did the next one, really. Sal inhaled them like they were made of oxygen instead of calories, and even Nova looked impressed as he held out his paper plate for a third slice.

"It's good," he said unrepentantly, earning a blush from her.

"Can't argue with that."

He did slow down after that, full, happy, and entirely content. Funny, after so much of his life spent having everything and still being unfulfilled, he felt the closest to satisfaction while sitting on a blanket in the grass.

Nova finished up her slice and leaned against him once again, sinking back into enjoying the setting sun. Sal was happy to watch it as well, until a question rose up in his mind.

"Nova?"

"Hmm?"

"Why did you ask me out?" He wasn't complaining. Far from it. But as far as he knew, he'd gone from the doghouse to being in her arms. Sure, he'd interfered with some ne'er-do-wells, but that was about it. He had thought that he'd broken her trust and forever ruined his chances of having something with her.

Which was a shame, because it took that stolen kiss for him to admit to himself that he wanted something from her at all.

"I think that's obvious," she said with a sort of huff, her cheeks coloring pink.

"Do you? Because I don't at all."

She twisted in his lap to look at his face. "Really?"

"One of the top ten mysteries of the world."

She laughed. "Alright, well. I asked you out because you make me laugh. Because I have so much fun with you that I somehow forget about all the stressful things in the world. I asked you out because I've been alone for so long—even when I lived with my family—that I got used to it. But when I'm with you, I remember what it's like to be with someone who likes my company."

His throat was constricting tightly, and he could feel his eyes starting to burn. "Huh, and here I thought this was all some ploy to get closer to Mom."

He meant it as a joke, a good way to deflect from the over-whelming surge of emotions inside of him, but Nova just took his face in her hands and stared up at him with all the honesty in the world.

"I like your mum a whole lot, because she makes me feel like there's not something wrong with me, and like I could have a home. But I asked you out for *you*, because you make me feel like anything can happen. You make me *happy*."

Those emotions bubbled up and he crashed his lips to hers again. She kissed him back until it felt like he wasn't going to burst.

"Why'd you say yes to going on a date with me?" Nova

whispered when they broke apart, her red lipstick smeared around her mouth just like he thought it would. Carefully, he brought his thumb up to wipe it away as he traced those beautiful lips of hers.

"Because I think I could be in love with you, and I'll take every chance that I can to see if I can somehow get you to fall in love with me too."

She went bright red at that, her eyes darting away. For a moment Sal thought that he had gone too far, but then her chocolate gaze returned to him. "Good call, because I think I might be halfway there already. Is that crazy?"

Somehow his heart kept beating, but barely. "Probably not as crazy as I am."

"Sounds like it might work out then."

"Yeah, it might." He was caught up in another wave of desire and happiness and all of those spinny emotions that made his words go slack, so he just kissed her again. Pouring everything he had into it. He did manage to stop himself before getting too carried away, however, and rested his forehead against hers.

"Hey, Nova," he rasped, heart thundering.

"Yeah?"

"Would you like to go on a date with me?"

She laughed and peppered his face with tiny, red-smeared pecks. "I thought you'd never ask."

Sal joined in her mirth, shaking his head, then returning her pecks. He didn't have even the slightest idea where he would take her, but he already knew he was hooked.

EPILOGUE

One Year Later

Nova

"*H*appy Anniversary, Nova. Sorry that Silas and Teddy kind of threw a wrench into our original plans."

Nova flushed, looking across the table to her boyfriend of one full year. He looked dashing in his collared shirt and dress pants, but then again, he always was handsome.

"They didn't know it was when we were planning our dinner. Besides, it's only once you get to throw a surprise engagement party."

"Well, hopefully once in a lifetime."

"Fair point there. That's certainly hope."

It had been a full year since she had asked him out, and life hadn't stopped running since. Mum Miller was ecstatic, of course, and already introduced Nova as her fourth daughter. Frenchie seemed pretty jazzed about it, as well, and asked Nova if she wanted to come to some of the occupational and support groups that she ran to rehabilitate youth who were disadvantaged or even homeless.

And Elizabeth had been loading her up with more and more work as she stayed on the ranch, trusting her with things that were a step beyond the scope of a vet tech, but Nova was thrilled about it. She was learning *so* much. If she continued to save up, she was pretty sure she could try the whole vet school thing again in a couple of years. She could probably go to part-time then, although she was still working out the budget for it.

"You ready to head to your apartment and open presents?" he asked.

Oh right. When Sal had visited her for the first time, he'd been appalled by her apartment building. That had led to a disagreement, with Nova feeling like she was being judged and Sal worried about her safety. In the end, they were able to see more eye to eye, but the last thing Nova had expected was for him to show her a newer, bigger, and more up-to-date apartment on her birthday and offer to pay the lease in full for her there and at her old place.

She'd almost refused, at first, because it was *so* much, but then he'd asked her to let him do something for her that mattered, and she'd happily given in. Sal was funny like that. Ever since he'd started to examine himself, he always did so much for everyone around him.

"Sure, since you already cheated and found yours," she said.

He grinned at her with that same charming smirk that always made her want to get into trouble. He was dangerous, that Miller boy. "Go easy on yourself. It's pretty hard to hide a horse big enough for me to ride."

"You're not kidding on that."

He came around the table, offering her his arm, and they left the expensive restaurant. It was one that Sterling recommended, saying it was one of his favorites and getting an elbow from Elizabeth. Nova didn't quite understand the joke, but there was definitely one between that couple about the place.

The drive back to her place was only about fifteen minutes. She didn't live in the upscale part of town, but she didn't live in the slums of the city like she had before. It was a good compromise, in her opinion, as she got the feeling that Sal would have bought her a whole mansion if she let him. He spoiled her so.

They arrived and headed up the stairs, walking into her spacious flat where she saw the pastel gift bag he had left on her coffee table. Kicking her heels off by the door, she flounced over and plopped down.

Sal joined her, sitting more carefully. He'd only accidentally broken one of her chairs *once* and had insisted on buying her a sturdier couch that wasn't a curb-side special, but apparently the event had traumatized him because he always took his time whenever lowering himself onto her furniture.

All that self-improvement, but he was still a drama queen.

"Well, what are you waiting for?" he asked once he was settled.

Nova clapped her hands and snatched up the bag, opening it to reveal an envelope inside.

Huh.

That was... different.

"What is it?" she asked.

"An envelope."

"I know that," she retorted. "What's in it?"

"I guess you'll have to open it and see."

She did so, completely baffled at what it could be. It was too thin to be cash but too small to be much else.

But then she spotted the telltale routing number, and within another moment a check was in her hands. A check for *way* too much.

"I..."

Sal was normally so romantic with his gifts, so thoughtful, so it didn't seem like something he would do.

"I don't understand," she said, looking at him.

"I don't think you realize it, but you've mentioned a few times how you always wanted to finish your schooling for being a vet once you got on your feet. I've been wanting to do something impactful, and it seemed like a good place to start." For some bizarre reason, he looked nervous. "So, I suppose you can consider yourself the first recipient of the Salvatore Miller Scholarship."

Nova's mouth fell open. Words probably should have come out of it, but there was just silence. She snapped it shut, swallowed, tried again, but could only let out a strangled sort of noise. Words. She needed *words*.

"I don't know what to say," she gasped out finally.

"That's alright," Sal said, moving closer to her. His giant hands wrapped around hers, as comforting as ever. "I want to support you because I believe in you and everything you can do. You'll be an amazing vet. And, maybe it's selfish, but I can't help but feel kinda responsible for all the people you're going to make happy."

It was so much. It was *too* much. And yet it was so utterly perfect that all she could do was throw her arms around him and hug him for all that she was worth.

"Thank you," she said, tears streaming down her face. "Thank you, thank you, *thank you.*"

"Don't worry about it," he said, those strong arms cradling her as usual. She still loved those embraces as much as she had in the beginning. "Happy anniversary, Nova."

She kissed him senseless, and maybe she was a bit senseless too, breaking away from him eventually to look down at the check again. It was happening. It was happening! She was going to be a vet.

"I can't believe this. This bumps up everything by years! It's amazing."

"Hopefully it didn't ruin too much of your timeline," Sal said with a wry smile.

But she was too happy to care. "I mean, our wedding might have to wait until I'm a doctor now so it can be on our official marriage certificate, but that's about the only thing I can think of."

She realized exactly what she said about thirty seconds after she said it, freezing in his arms. Glancing to Sal, she saw that he certainly looked shocked.

Oh no! She should know better than that!

"S-sorry! I was just talking. I—"

But then his hands came up to hold her face, his eyes locking onto hers. "Nova Clark, do you want to marry me?"

It was tempting to lie and say no, only because she was embarrassed, but she couldn't lie to Sal. Not when he had always been so honest with her.

"Of course. You're the love of my life. I know it the same as I know how much I want to be a vet."

He beamed at her, so blinding that she was stunned. Letting go of her face, he checked his watch. Apparently, he liked what he saw, because he was still grinning when he addressed her again.

"You know, it's early enough that we can go get some ring shopping in if we want."

Her eyes went wide, and she knew it. "What? Are you serious?"

"I don't think I've ever been more serious."

She kissed him again, pouring her all into it and leaving them both breathless. "Does that answer your question?" she shot back; her grin almost as broad as his.

"You bet," he said, standing and offering her his hand.

Nova took it, more excited than ever for the next step of their journey together. It looked like there was another exciting announcement to make before Sterling and Elizabeth's wedding in the summer. After all the drama at Solomon and Frenchie's winter wedding, the younger twin had chosen to switch things up.

But that was the thing about the Millers, there was always something impossible and wonderful and revolutionary happening.

Nova couldn't wait to experience all of that for the rest of her life.

∼

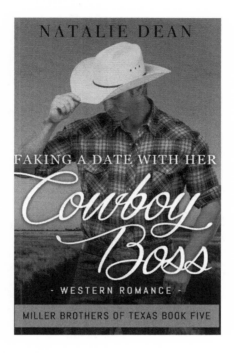

HELLO READER! I hope you enjoyed Salvatore and Nova's love story. It's time for the final Miller Brothers of Texas story. This love story has a little bit of pretend dating going on, but only so that Simon can protect Leilani from her past. With that protection comes a bit of romantic suspense alongside the sweet romance we all love.

You can find Simon and Leilani's love story on all major retailers. But of course, as previously mentioned, it sure would be great if you could support my small bookstore. Scan the QR code below to be taken to Faking a Date with her Cowboy Boss at Natalie Dean Books. If scanning QR codes isn't your thing, you can also find my store here: nataliedeanbooks.com Just look under the Miller stories tab for Miller Brothers of Texas, and you should find this book.

ABOUT THE AUTHOR

Born and raised in a small coastal town in the south, I was raised to treasure family and love the Lord. I'm a dedicated homeschooling mom who loves to travel and spend time with my growing-up-too-fast son.

When I'm not busy writing or running my business, you can find me cleaning house, cooking dinner, feeding our three rescue cats, trying to make learning fun and coaxing my son to pick up his toys. On less busy days, you may also find me paddling down a spring run in Florida, hiking a mountain trail in Georgia (on the rare vacation to the mountains), or enjoying a book.

If you love Natalie Dean books, you can be notified of new releases by signing up to my newsletter at nataliedeanauthor.com, where you will also receive two free short stories for signing up. Just click on the "Free Books" tab at the top and you'll be on your way!

Also, as previously mentioned, I've opened my own online bookstore and I'd love your support! As of June 2024, I'm selling my ebooks at Natalie Dean Books. By late summer or fall 2024, I should have audiobooks, regular paperbacks, large print paperbacks, dyslexic print paperbacks and signed paperbacks all available. At the request of my loyal readers, I'll also be adding merchandise, such as glasses, cups, magnets and more. So come check out my small mom-owned author business at nataliedeanbooks.com.

You can also scan the QR code below to be taken to the home page of Natalie Dean Books.

Made in the USA
Columbia, SC
15 December 2024

49531784R00140